JEANINE
ENGLERT

The Lost Laird
from Her Past

HARLEQUIN
HISTORICAL

HISTORICAL™

Recycling programs
for this product may
not exist in your area.

ISBN-13: 978-1-335-72328-4

The Lost Laird from Her Past

Harlequin Enterprises ULC
22 Adelaide St. West, 41st Floor
Toronto, Ontario M5H 4E3, Canada
www.Harlequin.com

Printed in U.S.A.

Jeanine Englert's love affair with mysteries and romance began with Nancy Drew and her grandmother's bookshelves of romance novels. When she isn't wrangling with her characters, she can be found trying to convince her husband to watch her latest Masterpiece/BBC show obsession. She loves to talk about writing, her beloved rescue pups, as well as mysteries and romance with readers. Visit her website at www.jeaninewrites.com.

Books by Jeanine Englert

Harlequin Historical

The Highlander's Secret Son

Falling for a Stewart

Eloping with the Laird
The Lost Laird from Her Past

Visit the Author Profile page
at Harlequin.com.

To my grandmother, Joanne.

You always made me feel like the most loved person in the world. Thank you for always reminding me that I was enough, even when I didn't believe it myself.

I love you and miss you.

He pulled her out of the carriage and quickly shifted out of its path, shielding her with his body.

Having removed his steadying weight, the wooden carcass of the carriage rocked and then careened past them down the hillside before crashing into the bottom of a ravine, splintering into bits. If he'd been seconds longer, they would have been crushed along the forest floor with it. He shook off the thought and continued, clutching the woman as tightly as he dared due to her unknown injuries. She smelled of lavender and rose... He stilled, arrested by the flash of memories the fragrance provoked.

He breathed in again. His body tightened in longing. He shifted her in his arms, desperate to get her face in the moonlight for a better look. It couldn't be... Could it? Surely time was playing tricks on his senses and crushing fatigue confused his mind. His heart pounded, his mind demanding to know if his fear was true. Finally, a cloud passed, and the moonlight allowed him to see her more clearly.

Lord above.

The sight of her landed a solid punch to his gut and his legs tingled. He froze on the hillside and stared down at the woman in his arms as his heart slammed into his chest.

"Brenna?" he asked. "Is that you?"

Author Note

The Lost Laird from Her Past picks up a year and a half after the end of *Eloping with the Laird* in the wintry Scottish Highlands near Loch Linnhe. Garrick MacLean has returned home after being away for over a year. The once strong, confident soldier is battered and beaten down by life and struggling to find his footing in the new situation he is now forced to live with.

Brenna Stewart is wavering in her own decisions about her future. She is determined to find her worth but uncertain of how to go about it. All she knows for sure is that she has never felt like she was enough.

This book is for everyone who has ever believed they were too lost to find their way home, or too undeserving to find their way back. Remember home is a part of you and that you are never too broken to be loved.

Wishing all of you peace and serenity.

Chapter One

Road to Westmoreland, near Loch Linnhe, Scotland, November 1743

The acrid smell of smoke filled the air as Garrick Mac-Lean, Laird of Westmoreland, reined in his horse and crested the final steep incline on the dirt road to his home just beyond Loch Linnhe. The grey puffs buffeting amongst the rising full moon blocked his view of the majestic profile of Westmoreland, giving him a longer reprieve from facing the painful truth seeing his ancestral home would rouse in him. That he had failed his family and failed in his duty as laird to protect his sister.

As his horse climbed, Garrick slid back in the saddle. The cool weight of his sister's silver crucifix pressed against his neck where it hung from a loose chain. The solitary heirloom was a heady reminder of what he had lost and of what little he could bring to his mother to grant her peace. He knew it would be no comfort, but he had nothing else to give. At least his sister, Ayleen, had been buried in the place she had given her life to protect, even if he hated God for it.

The smell of smoke intensified and heat flushed his limbs as it triggered the memory of his arrival in Perth a year ago in search of his sister...

'Ayleen!' Garrick yelled at the burning abbey. He ran towards the structure and hit a wall of heat and flame he couldn't pass. He jogged alongside it, searching for an opening, any opening, in the fire.

His heart sank. There wasn't one.

Panic screeched along his limbs. What if he was too late?

He heard a scream and turned.

Ayleen.

Reivers had her. Their faces were covered in blood and etched in cruelty and hate. She was kicking, flailing, and trying to fight them off. He froze, his legs tree trunks he couldn't move, his limbs stone. She met his gaze and smiled at him, the relief at seeing him evident in her eyes.

His chest tightened but still he couldn't move. He just stared and her smile faltered.

'Garrick!' she yelled.

Finally, his legs gained feeling and he ran to her. A reiver sank his blade into her gut and fled. Agony rippled along her face and her eyes closed as she crumpled to the ground. Garrick ran and ran, skidding to her in the grass on his knees. Please be alive. Please, Ayleen. *Scooping her up into his arms, he knew his*

*prayer had been discarded. She was dead, her eyes
wide and staring into the heavens above.*

*His scream burned his throat. What had he done?
He could have saved her, but he'd done nothing. When
it had counted most, he'd frozen.*

*'I'm sorry, sister,' he whispered in her ear as he
rocked her in his arms. 'I failed you.'*

Garrick shifted on his mount, clutching the reins to
smother the tremble in his hands as well as the shame
and horror of that day. If he'd not encouraged her to
follow her heart and calling to the church, but had arranged a marriage for her as he should have as her
older brother and laird of the clan, his sister would still
be alive. Perhaps even happily married with her own
bairn by now, and he an uncle. His gut tightened and
he ground his teeth. Only fools followed their hearts.
He knew that now.

Yet another reason it should have been him rather
than his elder brother Lon to die of fever years ago.
Garrick didn't know how to be laird, just as his father had long suspected. His heart was too soft, his
feelings too deep. But not any more. He'd learned his
bloody lesson.

His dark stallion continued its steady plodding along
the dirt road and Garrick attempted to shake off the
ghosts of regrets surrounding him. Dusk pitted the sky
with shadow and the Highlands began to hide her secrets, one of the things she did best. He flipped up the
collar of his overcoat to block the wind from his neck
and shifted from the road to the grass to avoid the

slick pockets of ice shimmering in the gouges of the worn road. The crunch of the frozen stalks beneath his horse's hooves was a signal December was near. The budding winter winds and first snows of the season would press mercilessly upon them in the coming weeks.

Not much had changed within the villages and towns he had passed on his return from Perth, but he had. When he'd left Westmoreland over a year ago, he'd believed himself invincible, and that his will alone would help him rescue his sister from the bloody skirmishes along the Borderlands, but he'd been wrong. He'd arrived too late to protect her from the heartless reivers who had risen like ash from the forsaken land and destroyed it once more. Nothing had been the same since.

As Garrick began to descend, he spied the shell of an overturned carriage resting precariously along the grassy slope of the glen below. He narrowed his gaze. Flames licked down the sides of the wide wooden frame as the fire burned itself out. Empty horse tethers rested along the ground. Gooseflesh rose along his skin. Something wasn't right. He slackened his hold on the reins, scanning from left to right, his gaze sweeping methodically over the scene as it would on a battlefield. Caution and instincts kept a man alive, not weaponry. He'd learned that early on.

When he spied a shadowy mound at the edge of the path half covered in grass and overgrowth, Garrick guided his mount to a stop. It could be part of a planned ambush. Or it could be a wounded man in need of assistance. There was no way to know until he got closer. Shifting the reins to one hand, he pulled a dirk from his waist belt. So much for an uneventful return home this eve.

He dismounted, tethered his horse to a small sapling nearby and approached, his eyes fixed on the dark form, the edges of it sharpening into focus with each step closer. His heart picked up speed. The man had been cleaved in the chest and gut and stripped of anything of value. He was sprawled without shoes or coat like a large X upon the ground. The awkward and unnatural twist of his limbs left little doubt. He was dead.

What Garrick had first thought an accident from afar now appeared otherwise. He scanned the area and found another body in the grass not far away from the first. It looked as if the man had attempted to outrun his attackers, to disappear into the glen and forest below for cover. The man hadn't got far but had been downed by a single blade to the back by a skilled thrower, or perhaps a man schooled to kill quickly, as he was. Garrick turned the body over and cursed. The lad looked the age of his younger brother, Cairn, who was scarce old enough to take a blade to his cheek.

The boy's wide, glassy brown eyes stared back at him, unseeing and full of fear. *Poor lad*. He'd not been dead long. His limbs were still floppy and loose. Garrick guided the boy's eyelids closed with his hand, saying a brief soldier's prayer for a quick release of his spirit to peace. He sighed. Such a loss for no reason. Years ago, he might have felt a twist of anguish in his gut at the sight of the dead boy. Now, he accepted it as a part of existence. The Highlands had changed, England had changed and he had changed along with them. He wasn't the same man who had left this hillside over a year ago, full of certainty for his future.

Now he was certain of…nothing.

A noise stilled him. He paused and listened, closing his eyes to determine the direction of the sound. A soft whimpering, almost like a gentle mewling from a wounded animal seized his ears and he held his breath, concentrating on only the plaintive cry. He opened his eyes. It was coming from the carcass of the overturned carriage that still smoked. He crossed the road with his dirk poised and ready.

He slid down a patch of slick grass and landed on a bevy of boulders that appeared to be holding the carriage in place. Careful to avoid the weak, winking flames, he peered through what was left of the window of a once fine carriage. He could smell and see the remnants of black varnish paint and the faint outline of a gold crest on the door.

He frowned. Such finery wasn't often seen in the Highlands this far north, and the fools within had made themselves a target by travelling so late and without adequate protection. People in the Highlands were desperate, hungry and willing to take what they needed these days. Moonlight winked against the shattered glass, glittering along an ice-blue silk gown. He sucked in a breath.

Deuces.

There was a woman inside. Why had she been abandoned? He froze. *Unless she was dead.* He shoved the thought aside. He sheathed his blade and yanked on the carriage door, but it was jammed shut. Cursing under his breath, he rammed his shoulder into it once, then twice, until the wood gave way, splintering from the force. The carriage yawned under the shifting weight and threatened to roll down the hill, crushing them both. He leaned his weight against it and forced himself half inside. He'd not leave her to be scavenged by animals, even if she was dead.

The woman appeared lifeless, but the moaning from her lips convinced him otherwise. *Saints. She was alive.* His heart picked up speed. Westmoreland was not far. If he rode hard, he could be there in less than an hour. Bloody, dark, matted hair from a head wound obscured part of her face, but otherwise she seemed unharmed. Perhaps he could save her yet.

Sliding his arms around her torso and the billowing folds of her silk skirts, he scooped her up as he held the weight of the carriage at bay using his leg. She snuggled against him and wrapped an arm around his neck. The feel of her faint whisper of breath along his cheek awakened a small seed of worth and want in him. After a very long time of not feeling needed by anyone, and falling short of those who had, it filled him with a sense of purpose. Maybe he could save her, even if it had been far too late for him to save his sister.

He pulled her out of the carriage and quickly shifted out of its path, shielding her with his body. Without his steadying weight, the wooden carcass of the carriage rocked and then careened past them down the hillside before crashing into the bottom of a ravine, splintering into bits. If he'd been seconds longer, they would have been crushed with it along the forest floor. He shook off the thought and continued, clutching the woman as tightly as he dared due to her unknown injuries. She smelled of lavender and rose… He stilled, arrested by the flash of memories the fragrance provoked.

The woman's size and hair colour were familiar.

He breathed in again. His body tightened in longing. He shifted her in his arms, desperate to get her face in the moonlight for a better look. It couldn't be, could it? Surely time was playing tricks on his senses and crushing fatigue confusing his mind? His heart pounded, his mind demanding to know if his fear was true. Finally, a cloud passed and the moonlight allowed him to see her more clearly.

Lord above.

The sight of her landed a solid punch to his gut and his legs tingled. He stared down at the woman in his arms as his heart slammed into his chest.

'Brenna?' he asked. 'Is that you?'

There was no answer but that of his heart. He knew it was her, as he knew this road and the smell of the Highlands in winter—the pert tip of her nose, the single mole along her neck and the feel of her in his arms. But how could it be? She lived south-west of here at Glenhaven with her father and brother. And who were these men escorting her? Where was her chaperone, and why weren't Laird Stewart's men guarding her? He gently pushed back some of the matted hair from her face. None of it made any sense.

'Wake. You must wake,' he pleaded, gripping her face to rouse her.

I cannot lose you twice.

He leaned down to kiss her cheek but checked himself and pulled away in time. He didn't dare.

It had taken all of his strength to let Brenna go the first time. And he'd done so with calculated and deliberate force after Ayleen's death, when he'd realised he couldn't truly protect anyone or be of use to her as a husband. He'd not sent word to Brenna, as he'd promised when he'd left, had but stayed away long after he'd planned to return.

He'd enlisted his honed skills as a soldier to fight along the Borderlands. It suited him far better than his new role as laird, and he knew that. Rage had fuelled every cut of his blade into the enemy, and with each death he'd been able to pull back further into his armour as a warrior and away from his life in the Highlands. He was good at killing. Good at detaching. At least, when it didn't matter. When it mattered, he choked and did nothing, as he had with Ayleen. And, as the days and weeks had ticked by, the old Garrick had fallen away like an old skin shed by a snake.

He'd wanted Brenna to believe him dead and seek out a new life without him, and the only way to do that was to disappear from them all. Should he have written to her and helped her let go of any hopes she still had in him and their future? Aye, he should have. But he'd not been strong enough to lie to her and pretend he didn't still care for her. So, rather than lie, he'd denied himself all feeling and attachment to her, and it had worked. For the most part, anyway.

He'd been a coward. Yet another thing to hate himself for. He'd add it to the bloody list of his failings that was becoming as long as a scroll. He was no longer the man that could love, cherish and protect Brenna for the rest of her days, as he'd believed but a year ago. He'd given up any hopes of a future with her the day he had lost his sister. Brenna deserved to live the happy and full life he had once promised her with a man who could protect her.

His chest tightened. Even if such happiness rested with another man.

She didn't wake or move. Panic clawed along the edges of his spine. He had to get her care. And quickly. Who knew what additional injuries she might have sustained other than her head wound? The gulf between them now didn't matter, only her life.

If he could save her, he could redeem some small part of the man he'd once been and make up for the pain he had caused her this past year. All he needed to do was maintain his distance. He'd done so for a year already, and he'd have to face her soon enough. Once she was at Westmoreland, he would send word to her family. They would come to collect her and then they could continue on without one another, as he'd planned.

No doubt she would be filled with ire at the sight of him alive. And he would use her rage to maintain their estrangement. He deserved her hate and disdain.

He carried her to his stallion and rested her across his mount before untying the reins from the small tree. Then he gently pulled up behind her, readjusting her in his arms with an extra tartan wrapped about her for warmth and protection. She was chilled to the bone.

Who knew how long she'd been exposed to the elements?

He held Brenna tightly and rode as fast as he dared to Westmoreland. The sharp wind in his face was an intoxicating reminder that he was alive, as was she, and that all was not lost.

Not yet, anyway.

Chapter Two

Brenna Stewart woke and had an immediate desire to retch, yet she was too exhausted, and the pounding in her head demanded she keep still with her eyes closed. But all the jostling, all the blasted jostling which would not cease, made the nausea worse. *Curses.* She clutched her head, wincing from the pain. Where was she? A flash of a memory of fire startled her, breaking through part of her confusion amidst the fog of her mind. But it faded away before she could seize upon it, like water running through her fingers.

The harsh smell of damp earth, horse and smoke surrounded her, and she stifled a gag. 'Arthur?' she asked in a raspy voice, trying to clear her burning throat. A wave of dizziness threatened and she clung to his coat sleeve. Perhaps something had happened to the carriage, for she was on horseback now, she was sure of it. But why? And why could she not remember how she'd got here?

'Arthur, stop the horse,' she pleaded in a thready voice that sounded little like her own.

'Nay, I cannot. You're hurt. Be as still as you can. We must get you care.'

She froze. That wasn't Arthur. Yet, the voice sounded so familiar. She clawed through her mind to find the name but couldn't. She concentrated and was finally able to open her eyes and attempt to peer up through the mounds of tartan wrapped around her. She pressed her fingertips to her temple to stop the throbbing and discovered the bloody wound there. She hissed out a breath from how tender it was to her touch. No wonder her head ached.

'Blast,' she mumbled, trying to push herself up and away from the man who was definitely not Arthur for a better look at him. Had she been kidnapped?

'Best save your energy for something other than curses, Brenna.'

She stilled. She *knew* that voice. Even in a wave of confusion, his voice anchored her, as it always had. But it couldn't be, could it? He was dead. She fumbled her way through the wool covering her. Finally it gave way, and a strip of moonlight revealed the rugged, familiar shadowy profile of a man, a man she had once loved. She sucked in a breath. Gripping the horse's mane, she turned closer to him for a better look. Everyone had believed him dead, including her, but here he was. Alive.

'Garrick?' she asked, still uncertain if her injuries and confusion filled her vision with delusions and memories of the past.

'Aye,' he answered. 'Glad to see you awake. Who

is Arthur? And why were you travelling without your father's men? You could have been killed.'

'You are not dead.'

He met her gaze. 'Nay,' he answered. His words were flat, lifeless things floating in the air.

'Am *I* dead?' she asked. It sounded more logical than being here in his arms after so much time had passed without a single word. After long believing him dead. After grieving him for months and forcing herself to move on and let go of her hopes and dreams of their life together.

'You are alive, as am I.'

'You've been gone over a year without a word. Where have you been? Why did you not write?' Shock drowned out her logic and reason.

They continued on in silence.

'I did not think I needed to.' His words chiselled through her confusion. She stared at him blankly as a muscle worked in his jaw.

'After all this time, *that* is all you have to say to me?' she asked. Her joy at seeing him alive and confusion over his manner with her quickly gave way to anger. She swatted him on the shoulder.

She stared up at him. His strong profile, chiselled features and prominent Adam's apple were so familiar. Dizziness made her body sway and he steadied her.

'Best you lean back against me before you topple off. You've a head injury.'

'Where have you been? Why did you not write?' she demanded, the fog of her mind cleared by her frustration. 'Why did you not let me know that you were alive and well?'

He stared off into the distance.

His silence lit her ire like dry tinder. 'You will answer me,' she demanded.

'It was for the best for you to be without me. It still is.' His words chipped away at her understanding of the world.

'What? We loved one another. We'd planned to marry. How was allowing me to believe you were dead and grieving you for the best?'

'Perhaps you can tell me who you were travelling with. And why. Only a fool would travel in such finery around these parts so late without guards.' His words cut through the night air.

Fool? She pushed away from him to lash out, but the world flipped over on itself. She settled herself back against him until the spinning stopped.

'Where are Arthur and his son?' She'd try a new tack to get him talking. Something that would help her get the easier answers. Such as where she was, how she'd got here and what had happened to them on their journey. She'd get to why he'd abandoned her and allowed her to believe he was dead later.

If she didn't throttle him before then.

'The men travelling with you?'

'Aye. Where are they? Answer me,' she demanded, a wave of panic washing over her at the thought of something having happened to them.

He said nothing.

'Where are they?' she asked again.

He shifted on his mount and avoided her gaze. She felt for his trews, found the spot behind his knee that she could reach and pinched him. Hard. Just as she used to when he'd tried to keep a secret from her.

'Saints be,' he cursed and grabbed her hand. 'Stop.'

'Then tell me. Now.'

He hesitated and sighed. 'They're dead. I wanted to wait until you had rested and been tended to before I told you.'

She froze. *Dead?* 'How? What happened to them?'

'I don't know what happened, but they were killed. I found your carriage overturned on my way to Westmoreland. All were dead except for you.'

How in the world could Arthur and his son be dead?

Her ears buzzed, then a deafening silence. Then slowly came back the clomping of the horse's hooves, the feel of her lungs rising and falling and the tingling of her fingers.

Guilt assaulted her and she gagged. She covered her mouth and another dry retch seized her as she clutched the plaid to try to hold on.

He slowed his horse. 'Easy,' he offered, pressing a strong hand to her back while holding her arm to steady her.

'I shouldn't have asked them to take me. I should have known better.' Tears threatened and anger burned the back of her eyes. Making a muck of things seemed one of the only things she was truly good at, and she hated it.

You always were useless, Brenna. This union has great import. Stop asking questions about Mr Winters

*and do your duty, like your sister and your brother, by
securing this arrangement. Be pleasing and obedient.
If you cannot do such, then leave me be.'*

The memory of her father's harsh words before she'd
left for Oban a week ago to meet with her now fiancé,
Mr Stephen Winters, sent a flurry of trembles through
her body. Why had she been in such a hurry to return
home? Now Father would truly be furious with her, and
with good reason. She should have heeded his soldiers'
advice and waited to return tomorrow morn. This was
all her fault.

Garrick held her, but at a distance, as if careful to
touch her as little as possible. Yet another man who
thought her distasteful and lacking. Otherwise, why
would he have abandoned her and pretended to be dead
to escape her attentions?

'It is not your fault,' he assured her. 'It appeared to
be an ambush. I have seen them before, and there is
nothing you could have done. You are lucky to be alive,
as I believe they left you for dead.'

She wiped at her eyes, clutching his shoulder to balance herself as another wave of nausea passed. 'I…'
she began.

You were always so useless.

She shivered again and squeezed her eyes shut to
will the loop of words to stop their dull echo in her
head. No wonder Garrick had not come back for her.
Father was right. She was useless, and now she had
caused two men to die. All because she wished to be
home and sleep in her own bed rather than stay in Oban
another night with the dull and disinterested Mr Win-

ters. In a half-day, she could have safely ridden back in the family carriage with the Stewart caravan of soldiers.

'Quiet,' he stated, and pulled his horse to a stop.

His body tightened and he stilled. She opened her eyes. Something was wrong.

After studying something that Brenna couldn't see for far too long, Garrick turned his mount, and she felt herself sliding away from him as he guided the horse down the hillside. 'Hold on to his mane,' he whispered. 'We have to hide. *Now.*'

She remembered that sharp edge in his voice that he used only when he was serious. She clamped her mouth shut and gripped the horse's neck tightly. Something *was* wrong. They hid behind a large cluster of trees and waited.

Soon she saw shadows, a series of dark forms casting protruding profiles against the night sky. They were above them on the main road. One, two, three men, that she could see. Were there more? She clutched at the horse's mane and held her breath even though her heart hammered unevenly in her chest.

'Can't have gone far,' one man said. 'Why didn't you check and make sure she was dead?'

'Probably is dead. A foolish waste of time trailing after them. Just let the sot bury the girl. Even these bastards deserve to bury their dead, especially a pretty one like her.'

She swallowed the fear crawling along her skin. *They were English.* And brutal, by the sound of it. Pain gnawed at her nerves as shock roiled through her. How close had she come to dying? Worse, Arthur and his son were already dead. If Garrick hadn't saved her, she would be as well. She gripped his forearm and he rested his hand on hers and squeezed.

The men turned their mounts in their direction and began a steady advance towards them. Brenna froze. Garrick pulled the tartan back over her to shield her from view.

'Stay here and hide,' he ordered.

She heard the swish of a weapon pulled from its sheath and the mount shifted as he slid off the horse. What was he doing? Was he leaving her? She peeked out from the plaid and frowned. He was approaching them, and he was outnumbered.

Just like Garrick. He'd not back down from anything. Except for love. Except for her. He hadn't fought for them. He'd let her go without as much as a word. He'd allowed her to believe he was dead, he'd been so anxious to be rid of her. How had she not seen it before? Had she imagined their deep attachment? She bit her lip to squelch the emotion welling within her. Had she driven him away somehow?

She wiped her eyes. Father was right. She mucked up everything. Why could she never do the right thing? Now her foolishness and need to come home early had cost two men their lives, and maybe even Garrick's now.

The clickety-clack crunch of hooves along the rocks grew louder, closer. Her heart pounded in her chest. Where was Garrick? She clutched the blanket over her face once more and her body trembled.

'Adams?' One of the men spoke.

'I see it,' the other answered.

'Could be the girl.'

'Aye.'

Footfalls edged closer and closer still. The horse shifted on its feet.

Anger and fear tangled within her.

What was she supposed to do now? Had Garrick left her as bait? *Where was he?* She shivered again and her breath came out in irregular spurts. She had no weapon and was still dizzy. What was he thinking? A groan and then a loud thud startled her, and she gripped the horse's mane. Was that Garrick or the other man? She peered out from the blanket and saw him battling two men, while a third lay splayed out on the ground.

Did he honestly expect her to stay here and do nothing when their very lives were at stake? *Blast.* Anger flushed her body. She'd not let Arthur and his son's deaths be for nothing. They deserved justice. Even if she didn't know how to fight, she could try. What did she have to lose now? She'd ruined everything already. She reached into the saddlebags, feeling for any sort of weapon she could find.

Finally, her hand closed over the leather-wrapped grip of a small dirk. She slid from the horse to the ground in a rather ungraceful flop and winced as she landed on her backside, covered in layers of blue silk. Once everything ceased spinning, she made her way through the cold, dewy grass on all fours, cursing her choice of dress as she dragged the heavy, soiled material behind her. The men battled as she crawled along the freezing ground. Once she was close enough, she sat back on her haunches, shut one of her eyes to try to focus the blurring forms into a single one and threw the blade. It hit the man in the back. She gasped and covered her mouth with her hand. He staggered forward before collapsing to the ground.

She didn't know if she was more shocked that she had hit him with the dagger at all or that she had killed him. Perhaps it didn't matter for, in the end, she'd saved them both.

Garrick knocked the other man out cold and then glared at her. 'What are you doing?'

'Helping.'

'Well, don't.' He stomped down the hillside, pulled her up to standing and supported her as they made their way back to the horse.

'You'd prefer I watch you get killed?'

'Aye. I'd rather that than *you* being killed.'

She shook her head. Perhaps she had been a bit impetuous, but it worked, hadn't it? Not that he would ever admit it. 'Just as mule-headed as you've always been.'

'You're one to say. You've suffered a head injury yet insist on thrusting yourself into a situation I clearly had in hand.'

'Did you?' she challenged, crossing her arms against her chest and lifting an eyebrow at him.

'Aye,' he griped, levelling his gaze at her.

He lifted her, plopped her unceremoniously on the horse and mounted behind her. He wrapped his arm around her waist, pulling her flush against his hard, muscular chest, before loosening his hold and sliding further back on the saddle as if he couldn't stand to be any closer. As the horse began its journey up the hill back to the main road, she wondered why she'd ever grieved this detestable man at all.

Chapter Three

'You could just say thank you,' Brenna grumbled.

Garrick would have preferred to swallow a handful of nettles. It didn't matter if she might be right. She exasperated him as finely as he remembered, and he clenched his jaw until it ached.

The woman could have got herself killed. And he couldn't lose anyone else. Why couldn't she understand that? The sooner he reached Westmoreland to deposit her for care under someone else's watch, the better. Until then, he'd try to understand how the hell she'd got herself into such a fine mess.

'Care to tell me why a band of English mercenaries are hunting you through the Highlands? And where you learned to throw a blade?' Garrick tugged the reins for his mount to set off for Westmoreland once more.

They were safe. For now.

'As much as I don't wish to admit it, the throw was luck. And mercenaries? How do you know that is who they were? There is no reason for them to be after us.

Perhaps we were just in the wrong place at the wrong time.'

'Mercenaries do everything with purpose. I've seen many similar scenes over the last year. It was intentional. You were targeted. I want to know why.' His words were tight and clipped. Anger and upset at almost losing her bubbled in his gut.

'I can't imagine why. Arthur and his son were merely bringing me back home.'

'Who are they? Why were you not travelling with your father's men with proper protection? Those men didn't look capable of protecting you. One of them was just a boy.'

Brenna squared her shoulder and shifted further away from him. 'Father selected a husband for me. He sent me south to meet with him one final time to settle the terms of our engagement and pending marriage. A Mr Stephen Winters. He divides his time between London, Edinburgh and Oban. His driver, Arthur, and his son agreed to take me back to Glenhaven this eve rather than tomorrow. They worked for him, this man I am to marry.'

Every fibre of Garrick's body tightened and ached. *Saints be.* She was to marry another man *and* he was English? How much could a man take? He shook his head. While he knew he'd purposefully and wilfully given up on the idea of marrying Brenna, knowing she was promised to another made jealousy bloom tight and full in his chest. And anger too. She had moved on quite easily from the idea of him once she'd believed he was dead.

'And what of us?' he asked. 'What of *our* understanding?'

'What understanding? We were not officially engaged. I waited for you, but you never came home. You never wrote. Nothing. It is as if you are a ghost returned from the dead. It's been over a year without a word from you to anyone. Not me, nor your family. What else was I and everyone else to believe?'

'As you can see, I'm not dead, nor a ghost.'

'Aye, here you are,' she added under her breath.

'What does that mean?' he asked, irritation sharpening the edge of his words once more.

Silence was his answer.

'Why did you not wait for me?' The words surprised even him as they fell from his lips. He'd intentionally let her go. He had no claim or demands he could make. Not really. Heat flushed his face. He sounded like old Garrick. Lovesick and hopeful.

It turned his stomach.

She scoffed, facing him. 'Wait! I did. It's been over a year. What were we all supposed to think, especially me? Should I have waited for ever?'

Aye.

But he knew it was a foolish and faulty answer. He'd let her go by not promising her something, by not writing to her—to anyone, for that matter—and he knew that. Each time he'd tried to put his heart on the page and pen such a letter to let her go, he'd batted the parchment into a ball and tossed it in the rubbish. He couldn't let her go, but he also couldn't face his shame.

He couldn't admit he wasn't the man she deserved. He still couldn't.

How could he tell her his sister was dead because of him? He hadn't been able to bear to tell his family or her of his failure. Then he'd stayed away because of guilt and had joined up again as a soldier, despite the duties he had as laird. And now? He didn't deserve happiness after all he'd done. Not any more. He'd killed too many, lost too much, and the colourful beauty he used to see in the world was now a fitful array of charcoal and grey.

'Answer me,' she demanded. Her words yanked him back to the present. Her eyes narrowed on him like a quiver, which he didn't like at all. He was not the one who'd gone and got engaged, now, was he?

'Why? Does it matter what I wished now? You have made your choice.' He shifted on his mount and grunted involuntarily before sucking in a pained breath.

She patted his forearm, and he winced, pulling away from her touch on instinct. He'd taken a blade to his arm, as well as his side during his struggle with the men, and they pained him like the devil. 'You're injured,' she stated, tugging up his tunic sleeve to reveal the wound.

'As are you,' he answered blandly. 'A fine pair we make.'

'We must stop. Wrap it, at least.'

'No time.'

'Wait. Where are we going?' she asked, scanning the road ahead. A thread of uncertainty unravelled in her voice.

'To Westmoreland. Where else would I be headed? I am finally returning to see my family. They can tend to you until your brother can collect you, and I can tell them of my journey.'

And that I failed my mission to rescue Ayleen and that she is dead. Because of me.

'You have not heard?' Her words were quiet and hesitant.

'About…?' he asked, his heart picking up speed in his chest.

She pressed a hand to his uninjured arm and turned in his hold to face him. 'Garrick, the King and his men seized Westmoreland. Your family isn't there.'

What?

He'd heard her words, but they were nonsensical. 'Why?' He chuckled. 'I don't understand. Where else would they be? Cairn wouldn't have just abandoned it without a fight. And mother…' The more he thought of it, the more he couldn't understand what Brenna was saying, and his fingers began to tingle.

'Let's stop for a moment. I…' The way she said the words and the sympathy in her eyes chilled his blood. His legs numbed. Gooseflesh rose along his arms.

'Tell me what has happened,' he demanded, bringing his mount to a stop.

She hesitated and he gripped her shoulders tightly, almost shaking her. 'You will *tell* me. Tell me all of it. *Now*,' he commanded, his voice sounding harsher than he intended.

'I… I don't wish to,' she stuttered, her voice just above a tremble. A single tear ran down her cheek.

He loosened his hold, closed his eyes and lowered his voice. 'Please. Tell me.'

Finally, she released a shaky breath and her light blue gaze held his. The emotion in it cut him to the quick. He knew her words would break him further. He prepared himself to absorb what he was sure would be a heavy blow.

'Your brother would not give in to the tax collector's demands. They were made an example of by the King's men. By the time we heard of the dispute and the outcome, it was too late for anyone to intercede.' She dropped her gaze and sniffed. 'I am so sorry. We all are.'

He swallowed and cleared his throat to ask the question he needed to. The one he dreaded. 'Are they dead?'

'Aye. It has been almost six months.' She worried her hands in her lap. 'Westmoreland was seized and many of the clan sought refuge with the Camerons and other clans farther north.'

He pressed his lips together and commanded himself to breathe and not scream in anguish. He would one day, but not now. Not while they were still in danger. While he didn't care much for his own survival, he did care for Brenna's. He always had. And now she was all he had left in this world. She could still live and be happy, unlike him, who had nothing and no one.

Not any more.

Moments ago, he'd only been bemoaning the loss of Ayleen. Now, he realised his absence from Westmoreland had cost him everything. What had remained of his clan, his family and his heritage, was now lost for ever.

Because of him. Because he hadn't been there to protect them. He'd been off wallowing in his shame and guilt over Ayleen, telling himself they were better off without him. How had he been such a fool once more?

He steeled his heart and pushed down his sorrow. How had this happened? All of them were dead. And he'd not been there for them as laird, brother and son. His throat ached, his chest squeezed and what grief he'd felt this morn was now compounded. By staying away, he had killed them all. What was he good for?

Nothing, it seemed.

He stilled.

Or maybe one last thing.

Purpose flared in him like a winking candle battling the breeze. He didn't have time to grieve. Keeping Brenna alive was now his sole focus. After that, he would have his revenge on those who had killed his family and scattered his clan to the ends of Scotland, or he'd die trying.

He sucked in greedy breaths to quell the rage and deep ache of regret filling his chest. After a few more moments of silence, he stared off in the distance, counting to slow his heart as well as his grief. It worked on the battlefield, so he hoped it might anchor him now. He could feel Brenna's gaze on him like the sun warming his face. He dared not meet it. Otherwise, he might crush her in his arms and seek the solace his soul craved. And, if there was one thing he no longer deserved in his life, it was her.

He tightened his jaw and clenched his shaking hands on the reins. He would keep his anger close for now. Feed on it and focus solely on getting Brenna home to Glenhaven safely.

Her life and happiness was all that mattered now.

Suddenly, a piece of logic slid into place for him. 'Is what happened to Westmoreland and my family why your father was in such haste to arrange a union for you with an Englishman?' Garrick asked as he tugged down his coat sleeves.

She nodded. 'He hoped it would offer us some protection after what happened to your clan. Father is ailing, and Ewan has not settled into his role as future laird yet.'

'Has your brother taken no wife?' Garrick could not keep the surprise from his voice. Ewan was well beyond the age for marriage, especially as the future laird of his clan.

'Nay. As you know, he has long been reluctant to tether himself to anyone, much to Father's annoyance.'

'I do remember that.' Garrick shifted the reins in his hands and stretched them.

'Aye. After losing Emogene, he fears making a poor choice, so he makes none.'

'And he has a right to fear such,' Garrick answered. He knew all about mistakes and regrets. One poor choice could haunt a person for a lifetime. And he seemed to be making one poor choice after another, with no end in sight.

'Where will we go?' Brenna shivered and rubbed her arms.

'Shelter for now. It is too dangerous to travel at night, especially if those men are still after you,' he answered.

Then, he'd return her to her family in Glenhaven. After that, he wasn't sure. He was now a man without a home or family. All he had left in the world was her, and he didn't have her at all.

Chapter Four

Brenna leaned back against Garrick as they travelled
across an open meadow into the cover of the edge of
forest that would lead them away from the road to
Westmoreland, and south towards her home of Glenhaven. How many times had she ridden up this final
stretch of road by coach eager to see Garrick emerge
from the castle doors, and ridden away with a twinge
of sadness on her heart for missing him before she'd
even exited the drive? Too many to count during their
courtship. Now, it seemed a painful reminder of all
they had both lost. The road didn't lead to anyone's
home any more.

Brenna struggled to fully sit up. Fatigue and her
throbbing skull made wakefulness a challenge for her,
but she didn't dare drift off. Arthur and his son Roland
were dead. Garrick had returned. The world she had
woken to this morn had flipped on end, and she had
no idea what would happen next.

She shifted forward to keep space between Gar-

rick and her, but the pull of her body to his and the
heat emanating from his solid, muscular frame made it
difficult. When he cinched his arm tighter around her
waist, she had no choice but to relax against him, and
the familiar warmth of his body pooled slowly through
her fingers and toes. Soon the chattering of her teeth
ceased, reducing the hammering in her head.

'Where have you been?' she asked, her words loud
against the backdrop of a rippling stream and a low
hoot of an owl. She had kept her question at bay as long
as her heart would allow. He'd just learned he'd lost his
family and his clan, and she should have heeded that
and waited for another moment, but her mind would
not let loose of its need to know and understand why
he had left and abandoned her.

Had they not been in love? She'd thought they would
live the rest of their lives together as man and wife and
build a family. But then he'd left to rescue Ayleen and
had never returned. No word, no letter, not a hint of
where he was or if he was even alive. She had grieved
him for months before giving in to Father's demands
for her to wed.

Yet now here he was, without a word of explanation.
She deserved an explanation at least, didn't she?
But he said nothing.

The horse crossed a bevy of water, splashing through
what would be iced over in a few weeks. They began
an ascent and her body pressed more tightly against
Garrick, causing his words to edge across her cheek
like an intimate whisper when he finally answered. 'It
might be easier to say where I haven't been. Here.' His

voice dripped with regret, but her own hurt at being left made her unable to let it drop.

'That much is obvious. Answer me. I deserve at least that, do I not?'

She felt his chest rise and fall against her back, and what might have been a curse escaped his lips. They slowed at the edge of a cave. He dismounted, drew his blade from his waist belt and handed her the reins.

'Wait here. If someone comes, ride to safety. I'll find you if need be.'

Before she could utter a word, he disappeared into the dark mouth of the cave. He was gone so long, she feared he had been swallowed by it. Finally he emerged, took the reins and guided his mount to a nearby tree. Close enough to a stream to get water, the horse walked over and drank its fill. Brenna rubbed the stallion's neck, revelling in the animal's simple satisfaction. If only she could be pleased so easily.

She turned and found Garrick staring at her, his eyes haunted and lost as they caught a shaft of moonlight. His breath coiled up into the air. He broke the moment and came to her, taking her hand to help her dismount. She landed and grabbed his wounded forearm by accident. He winced but held steady as she gained her footing on the uneven ground.

She relented on getting an answer. For now.

'We need to tend to your wound,' she said, gesturing to his arm.

'Aye. And your head. All in good time. Let us get settled inside first. While we can't build a large fire without attracting attention, it will be warmer in the cave away from the wind, and we've access to water from the stream.'

She nibbled her lip, narrowing her gaze at the dark mouth of the cave. 'Animals?'

He smirked. 'None. I checked. I remember what happened the last time we were in a cave.'

She chuckled and shivered. 'Aye. I still twitch at the thought of those tiny bats whizzing by my hair.'

'While we might encounter a shrew or two, we'll be fine.'

Would they?

She hesitated. He gestured for her to enter ahead of him.

'If you sit on the western side, you'll avoid the wind,' he offered as they walked into the dark, damp mouth of the cave. 'Stay here.' He left without another word.

She wrapped the wool tartan around her and let the dark, dismal space cocoon her. She knew she should be grateful, and she was. They were alive. She just wished she didn't have to spend the night here with Garrick. Alone. She wished Arthur and his son weren't dead. That Garrick's family and home hadn't been lost. That she could be brave and stick up for herself, like her sister Moira.

But wishes were empty, useless things young lasses clung to for hope and were not for her any more. Practicality would serve her best, and marrying Stephen Winters was the option that would provide her family and her the most favour with the King and the most protection going forward. Even if he was dull and not the man she'd once hoped to marry.

But Garrick didn't seem to be that man any more either. The man she'd known wouldn't have abandoned her. He would have fought for her, for them, for their future, and not hidden himself away.

Her eyes adjusted to the darkness as she sat at the mouth of the cave. Soon, Garrick entered carrying an extra plaid, his saddlebags and a small lit torch that he wedged between two rocks to illuminate their space. He unfurled the plaid and laid it out on the ground, and Brenna settled on it with her back to the cave wall. He sat beside her, dumped the contents of his saddlebags on the plaid and went through them. 'We've enough food for two to three days if needed, but we'll have to find some hay or a place for Montgomerie to graze.'

'You named your horse Montgomerie?'

He shifted items around and avoided her gaze. 'Aye.'

She nibbled her lip. 'For me?'

He didn't answer, which was all the answer she needed.

'Do you still remember the poem?'

'Nay. I've long since forgotten such foolish things. Have some dried meat.' He began to pack the saddle-bags with great care.

Her cheeks heated. Well, she had not. Alexander Montgomerie was her favourite Scottish poet and, while Garrick might pretend the name of his horse had little significance, she was not daft. He did everything with purpose. He was calculated and precise, as a soldier should be. He always had been. Even though many things about him had changed, she doubted that had. He had cared for her as she had cared for him, despite the chasm between them now.

She bit into the salty meat and forced herself to eat, as she'd not had a bite since breaking her fast this morn. They sat in silence and ate as a light rain began to fall. If it had been a year ago, the night might have been beautiful, intimate and romantic. Now, it felt almost unbearable to be sitting here beside him. She swallowed the last bit of meat, unable to taste it at all, and pulled her legs up hugging them to her chest.

Garrick ripped a strip from the plaid and held it out in the rain before kneeling before her. He reached for her chin, his calloused fingertips skimming her smooth skin, igniting a rush of heat, awareness and longing through her, and she flinched.

'I'll not hurt you,' he said, frowning at her. 'Your injury needs to be cleaned so I can assess its seriousness.'

She relented, facing him in the flickering light. He began to wash her temple with one hand while clutching her chin with the other, and that achingly familiar thrill her body had always felt from his warm touch spread through her until it became hot and bright. She gripped his wrist and he stilled.

'Did I hurt you?'

Aye. Over hundreds of days.

'Nay,' she lied, removing her hand and releasing a breath. She commanded her body to cease its intense response to his touch, but it was hard to unwind the tight coil of attraction to him she'd always had despite what he'd done. Even now he was still the most handsome man she'd ever known. Fine lines flared out around the corners of his pale green eyes, his sandy hair covering part of his face. She could remember the feel of the stubble on his cheeks against her fingertips, and the way he would sigh when she'd press her lips to his angular jawline.

How many nights had she dreamed of his face and prayed for his return? So many that her body ached for him even still, even now when she knew he had abandoned her. But it no longer mattered. The past was just that. Now, she was engaged to another, and Garrick had let her go. He was simply following his duty as a soldier by protecting her now. He didn't love her. Perhaps he never had.

Her stomach lurched at such a realisation, crushing the trill of awareness she'd felt moments ago from his touch.

'Are you finished?' she asked.

'Patience.'

Blast. She shifted under his hold, willing time to pass more swiftly.

'Tell me more of your journey,' he commanded, continuing to clean her wound.

'We were travelling from Oban back to Glenhaven. Mr Winters has shipping interests in that area, so Father agreed for us to meet there for our final terms of engagement, even though Father was too ill to join us. While he sent Stewart soldiers down to accompany me to Oban earlier in the week, they stayed to gather supplies for Father, and had a plan to travel home on the morrow. I was eager to return. Stephen offered his driver Arthur and his son to escort me home today in his carriage, so I could tell Father of the news that my marriage was settled. I hoped it might ease some of his worry to know it had been secured.'

She didn't add that she hadn't been able to bear to stay a day longer. Stephen was not exactly the doting, interested fiancé a woman dreamed of. He was arrogant and drear at best. She doubted he held any interest in her beyond her lineage. His union with her was an arrangement born of necessity to please the King, nothing more. He'd made that clear upon her latest visit.

At least she had made a decision to please Father. He had to acknowledge her worth and willingness to help him and her clan now. She could hardly wait to see the pride on his face when she showed him the finalised terms of her upcoming marriage. He would finally see her value, and she clung to that hope even now.

'Why Oban?' he asked.

'It was halfway between Glenhaven and where Stephen resides in Edinburgh half of the year. Father suggested it and Stephen agreed.'

Garrick frowned. 'Not quite halfway between the two, if you ask me.'

She nodded in agreement, and then winced as he touched a tender spot along her scalp. 'You know my father. He is formidable. Stephen also knew it was nowhere near halfway between the two, but he allowed Father to win that round of battle.'

'Did you see your sister and brother-in-law while you were visiting in Oban?'

'Nay. I knew Moira would not approve of the match. She does not know.'

Garrick stopped and met her gaze, lifting his brow to encourage her to continue. Brenna shifted and fussed with the tartan draped around her. 'Moira never gave up on the idea you would return.'

Nor did I. Not really.

But Brenna refused to concede such an idea aloud. It did not matter what she felt or wanted now. She had made her decision, and so had he.

Garrick nodded and returned his attention to her wound, albeit his touch seemed harsher now. 'Ow!' she said. 'I believe it has been rubbed raw. That is enough.'

He ignored her and moved her hair back. 'What about while you were on the road? Where did the men come from that attacked your carriage?'

'The weather was fine and I remember listening to Arthur and Roland chatting above on the driver's bench. The scenery rolled by, and I fell asleep to the lulling motion of the carriage. I woke to the sound of raised voices. When I peered out of the carriage window and enquired about what was happening, a man with a scarred face approached, opened the door and hit me before I could do anything. That was the last I remembered until I awoke on horseback with you.'

It didn't seem real. It was as if it had all happened to someone else, but it hadn't.

'Nasty gash you earned for your trouble.' He kneaded his fingers gently through her hair and her breath stuttered from his touch. 'And quite the egg-shaped lump. Do you still feel dizzy?'

'Nay,' she answered. 'Not like before. I think the food, water and rest has helped.'

'And you've no idea why they attacked?' he asked.

'I can't think of any.' She extended her open hand. 'The cloth?'

He shook his head. 'Let me rinse it and get more water. Then you can repay me for my efforts.'

She felt along her temple and winced. It could have been much worse. Perhaps it had been best that she'd not seen Arthur or his son on the road. Her pulse quickened. 'When can we return to collect Arthur and Roland? We can't just leave them there unburied.'

Garrick returned and sat in front of her. 'For now, we must. Those men might be still looking for you and watching the scene. They seemed eager to make sure you were dead. Perhaps they believed you could identify them.'

'Why would they care if they are just thieving?'

'Good question. I think a band of thieves wouldn't have been searching for you to make sure you were dead but would've moved on to their next target. That is why I believe they were mercenaries and hired for their trouble.'

She paused. He had a point. 'Do you think there are any more? You killed two of them.'

'If I oversaw an attack on such a carriage, I would have had at least five men. Two for lookouts and three for execution of the task. If that is the case with you, then that leaves three. The one I left unconscious but not dead, and the other two we didn't see.' He handed her the cloth, newly rinsed and soaked with water.

She gestured to him. 'You'll need to remove your coat and tunic.'

He hesitated.

'I have seen your bare chest before, if you remember.' Her cheeks heated at such memories, and she clutched the cloth tightly. 'Now is not the time for modesty. We're sleeping in a cave together, after all,' she added.

Slowly, he attempted to remove his coat but stilled, his face scrunched up in pain. 'Let me help.' She rose to her knees and eased the coat sleeve off. It was then she saw that the front of his tunic, not just his sleeve, was soaked in blood. 'Garrick! Why did you not stop so this could be tended to? I thought you had a mere cut to your arm. This wound to your side is sizeable.'

'I've had much worse.' He grunted, pulling the tunic off in one deft movement with his good arm. His breathing was laboured from the effort, and the wound began to ooze blood.

She scrambled, tore a strip of fabric from her shift and pressed it to his side. He sucked in a breath at the force of it and attempted to pull her hand away.

'If you don't leave me to tend to this, Garrick Mac-Lean, by all that's holy…' she muttered.

He chuckled and let his hand drop away. 'Forgot about the crinkle you get in your brow when you're riled up.' He stared at her, and the smile he'd shown but a moment ago fell away. 'I've missed it.'

She held his gaze, her pulse quickening from his words. *And I you.*

He cleared his throat, his neck flushing with colour as he looked away, as if he'd just realised what he'd said and regretted it.

'You'll not distract me with your flattery,' she added to break the current in the air between them. 'You need stitches to close this or you'll bleed to death.'

'And you'll be the one to do it, will you?' he challenged, still looking away.

She squared her shoulders. 'Aye, I will. Anything in your bag of use for that?'

'Unfortunately.' He sighed and moved the bag closer to her.

She smiled and rummaged through it with her unoccupied hand. When she spied the small kit, she opened it. 'Quite the medicinal kit you have here.'

'As a soldier, I learned to be able to tend to my own wounds or others under my care. Otherwise, one doesn't last too long in battle.'

She found the needle and thread and set it aside.

'Where have you learned such skills?'

'A woman in the village. She came to us after her own clan, the MacDougalls, had been relocated by the King and his men. Used to be a healer. I asked her to teach me. You could say that I grew weary of being useless.'

He balked. 'What are you talking about? You were never useless.'

'Wasn't I, though?' she asked, threading the needle and avoiding his gaze. 'I sat about that castle waiting to be married off. Moira had her interests in botany and herbs, Ewan spent time learning the duties of being a laird and I sat absorbed in gowns, bows and flirtations without a true care or interest in the world.'

At least, that was what Father always said.

Garrick gripped her arm. 'You were never such to me.'

'But not useful enough to return and lay claim to, was I?' She pulled her hand away. 'You might want to find a stick to bite on before I stitch this up. It will hurt like the devil.'

Chapter Five

Garrick bit down on the stick he'd found and groaned. While he'd oft dreamt of Brenna's touch on his skin while he'd been away this past year, this was not quite the caress he'd hoped for. Sweat beaded his forehead and upper lip with each movement of the needle in and out of his skin. *Deuces.* When he thought he couldn't take a moment longer, he felt her tug once more to tie off the stitching. Then her lips skimmed along his skin as she bit off the end of the thread. His body quaked from the feel of her lush lips on his bare flesh, and he sucked in a breath commanding himself to focus on their survival.

This was not the time to be distracted. Too much was at stake. Namely, Brenna's life.

Her fingertips lingered along his side, and he thought he might die from the combination of agony and bliss. 'Lord above,' she murmured. Her hand trailed along the raised scars puckering his body. He swallowed hard. They were a permanent memory of a time he'd like to forget. He clambered for his blood-stained tunic and attempted to shrug it on. He didn't want her sympathy.

'Let me help you,' she whispered, edging closer to him, guiding the fabric over and down his torso. He was shivering. From shock, her touch or the memory of that day of his injuries, he didn't know. Nor did it matter. He closed his eyes, began counting and took in deep breaths to slow the hammering of his heart in hopes it would also quell his trembling. She didn't need his weakness.

He slid back beside her to lean against the cold but solid cave wall. He would collect himself like he always did and move on. Feeling and remembering would not change the past. Those men were still dead. His sister was still dead. Hell, his mother and brother were dead, and most likely countless other men and women of his clan. All because of him and his bloody weakness. While he'd not thought it possible to despise himself more now than he had this morn, he did. He was responsible for more than just Ayleen's death now. His hands were soaked in blood and loss.

Brenna settled a blanket over both of them and sidled up to him, her side pressed against his own. He should have moved away, but he didn't. She was all he had to link him to the past. The only flickering flame of light left in his life. Although he didn't deserve her and wouldn't allow himself to love her, he needed some small seed of comfort at this moment to keep himself from screaming aloud in anguish and grief. He clenched his jaw and blinked back the emotion that threatened. He didn't deserve to live, but she did.

'Cold,' she whispered.

He thought about wrapping his good arm about her for a moment, but he didn't dare. He didn't trust himself. 'Staying together will help,' he said.

As will keeping my distance. But he couldn't have both. Not today.

Not ever, it seemed.

'What is our plan?' she asked.

A good question. 'We can't go to Westmoreland.'

'What of Glenhaven? Surely we would be safe there?'

'Aye,' he answered. 'It is the best and closest option to get you the care you need. We will have to stay here the night, though. Then, we can pack up in the morning and journey there. I'm sure your father will be thrilled to know I am alive,' he added dryly.

Brenna woke with a dull, pounding ache at her temple. She squinted at the winking rays of sunshine sparkling at the opening of the cave. Garrick's warm arm was wrapped around her back and shoulder, and she was snuggled against his chest with her arm draped across his waist. She should have moved. It wasn't decent. She snuggled closer instead.

Decency had got her nowhere so far. She'd done all that had been expected of her in her role as the youngest daughter of a laird. She had dressed well, been polite and preened herself to within an inch of reason to get the attention of the right men for Father's sake—all to end up here in a cave with the man she had once hoped to marry, while engaged to a man who by all

accounts would forget her name if it weren't a requirement. Stephen Winters had not been an impressive man
in any way when she'd met him. Truth be told, he was
a bit of a gomeral.

She snuggled closer to Garrick, savouring what
would most likely be her last time to do so. She smiled
at the steady, even rise and fall of his chest as he slept
and the solid, safe feel of him holding her. He'd always seen and valued her in a way others hadn't, and
she had believed he'd loved her. But how could you
love someone and not return? He'd allowed everyone
to believe he was dead, even her. Losing him had set
her adrift, and she'd grieved him and the dream of the
life she'd thought they share together. How had she
been so wrong? Why had she not seen the truth? That
he hadn't cared for her at all.

She shivered.

'I can almost hear you thinking,' he said, his voice
husky with sleep.

'How long have you been awake?'

'Just a few minutes. I stayed awake most of the night
to make sure we hadn't been followed. Drifted off for
a few hours in the early morn. Did you sleep?'

'Aye,' she answered, her mind still full of confusion
and uncertainty.

He rubbed her arm absently for a few moments and
then stilled, as if he realised he shouldn't be. He shifted
and sat up, removing his arm from her waist. The feeling of loss was instantaneous and made her body ache,
much to her chagrin. She shouldn't miss the touch of

a man who didn't want her or love her, but she did all the same.

'How long will it take us to get to Glenhaven?'

'Longer than I'd like,' he answered. 'We need to move before the sun is fully up. If you need to…' He gestured to the woods.

'Aye. I won't be long.'

'Don't go far,' he answered as he followed her out of the mouth of the cave, heading in a different direction for privacy.

The woods sighed around her, as if the ground was also waking slowly this morn. Dew dusted the plants that poked through the dirt of the forest floor, and a few lone birds hopped from branch to branch in search of food. A doe off in the distance was grazing along with its mate. Brenna finished her ablutions and headed to the trickling stream. The feel of the cool water on her hands and face refreshed her despite the early-morning chill.

A branch snapped behind her. 'You're quite a difficult woman to find. Although the dress did help. Not many blue silk gowns out here in the woods.'

She froze. *That voice.* It was one of the men who had been searching for them last night. She would recognise it anywhere. She curled her palm around a large rock and hid it in the dense folds of her gown. Her heart hammered in her chest, and she rose slowly, catching sight of Garrick out of the corner of her eye outside the mouth of the cave. He saw her and knew she was in danger.

She turned to the stranger and he grabbed her arm,

yanking her close to him. So close, she could see the wide, dark pupils of his eyes and the unmistakable hatred in them as well. But she didn't even know the man. Why in the world did he hate her so?

No matter.

She'd not wait to find out. She lifted the rock in her other hand and swung until it made contact with his jaw. He cursed and his hold weakened long enough for her to break free and run from him, but she wasn't fast enough in her thin slippers on the slick ground. He lunged for her legs and caught her ankle, which brought her crashing flat onto the cold, hard earth, knocking the wind out of her.

She squirmed, clutching at the dirt and moss to gain purchase as she struggled for air, but he dragged her back. Kicking hard, she connected with his shoulder and he let go. Before she could rise, a blade flew by her in a whish and the man fell to the ground.

Finally, her lungs filled with the cold morning air, and she gasped in relief. Panting for breath, she clutched the leaves, attempting to rise.

Garrick rushed to her, sliding onto his knees into the wet grass and leaves. He clutched Brenna's face in his hands. 'Are you hurt?' His eyes searched her own.

'Nay,' she answered. Her voice and hands shook. She'd almost killed a man. Again.

He released a breath and relaxed. 'What were you thinking? Why did you not wait for my aid?'

'I couldn't afford to wait. And I might have been

dead before you reached me.' She accepted his hand and allowed him to pull her up to standing.

He paled and she realised the error of her words.

Blast. 'I am sorry. I didn't mean…'

'You could have got yourself killed. *Again*.' He ignored her earlier implication and shook his head. 'Come on. We need to leave in case there are others, which I believe there are.' He grabbed her hand and tugged her along.

'Shouldn't we see if he has something on his person that might help us find out who he is and why he is after us?'

They rushed to the dead man and Garrick tugged at his coat. 'He's still alive, but barely.'

'Why are you after me?' she demanded.

The man smiled at her as blood oozed from the corner of his mouth. 'You'll know soon enough, lass. I'd hate to ruin the surprise.'

And with that he was dead.

Garrick cursed and let go of him. The man's body flopped back to the ground.

'You search the left side of him and I'll search the right,' he commanded. 'Quickly.'

'I can't help but notice that you have great ease with searching a dead man,' she said, staring hesitantly at the man's body.

Garrick stilled and said nothing.

Her cheeks heated. Why had she said that? 'I'm sorry. That was a foolish thing to say.'

'No matter.'

She tugged some papers and correspondence bound with a ribbon out of the man's coat pocket.

'You might want to look away for this next bit,' Garrick suggested. 'There's another place I need to look.'

She blushed and turned away. While she didn't know exactly where he was searching, she had a fine idea of the general area.

'Ah! As I thought. It doesn't matter if you're a mercenary, soldier or farmer. You use the same practice for subterfuge. Done?' he asked.

'Aye,' she answered and faced him, extending the papers she'd found in the man's pockets.

He added them to the small dark satchel he'd found. 'We'll put them in the saddlebag and look at them later. But, for now, we must go.'

Saints be.

She paused.

He watched her face. 'What?'

'I'm not sure we should go to Glenhaven.'

'Why not?' he asked.

She pointed to his hands. 'We could be putting my family in danger. That is the satchel Father gave me as a gift for Stephen. I gave it to him myself when I arrived.'

'Surely not? One satchel looks much like another.'

'Is there one gold piece and all of the rest silver?'

He tugged open the bag and poured the contents into his hand. One lone gold coin shone amidst a sea of silver ones.

'It could be a coincidence.' Garrick frowned at his own statement.

'You heard the man. He said I would know soon

enough why they were after me. That he didn't wish to ruin the surprise.' Her voice shook as she said the words.

'Let us go,' he whispered tugging gently on her hand. 'We'll work this out, but not here in the middle of the woods, out in the open. Come.'

She blinked back at him. None of it made sense—the carriage attack, these men hunting her and the pouch of coin from her father on the dead man's person.

Nothing made sense any more.

He tugged her hand once more. 'Trust me.'

Meeting his gaze, Brenna nodded. She didn't trust him. Not really. Not after all that had happened. But what other choice did she have? She was being hunted for reasons she did not know and by men bent on seeing her dead. Her family could be in danger or…

Her steps faltered at another idea that cropped into her head. Could her father be involved? But why? How? Neither theory made a whit of sense and the latter was beyond unsettling to think upon. She picked up her skirts with her free hand and kept up with Garrick's furious pace through the forest.

Her heart pounded in her chest as they climbed the small incline back to the cave. She packed up their meagre belongings and Garrick readied Montgomerie, who had been grazing along a tuft of grass off to the side of the cave. Brenna attempted to wipe some of the mud and blood from her gown but gave up and wrapped a wool plaid around herself instead. She stepped into Garrick's open palm as he offered to help boost her up and onto Montgomerie. He swung up easily behind her.

'Ready?' he asked.

'Nay,' she answered, unable to keep the tremble out of her reply.

'Neither am I, but we go anyway. We'll head south, but off the main road to Glenhaven, until we can stop to look at those letters and the pouch and we're certain it is safe to do so. We'll not risk putting your family in danger in case there are others still following us.'

'Aye.'

She glanced back at the cave and where the dead man lay amongst the morning sunlight and tried to work out why and how she'd even got to this place. How had a carriage ride home turned into this? And how had her father's pouch of coin ended up in the hands of a man trying to kill her?

She stared down at the small garnet ring on her fourth finger. This simple engagement to an Englishman to help protect her family was becoming anything but.

Chapter Six

The western Highland terrain was as unforgiving as his past, and Garrick slowed Montgomerie as they began a steep incline along the narrow, rugged pass that hugged the coastline of Loch Linnhe and would bring them into the outskirts of Glencoe and if needed on down to Oban to Blackmore.

Even during the day, it was a far more dangerous route, riddled with unforgiving climbs, shifting rocks and high winds, but a less travelled one. They had a better chance travelling this route than the main road where they might encounter more men still looking for them. If they could reach Glenhaven in a day's time, they would be safe but, if they ended up needing to travel to Oban to seek refuge with Brenna's sister and brother-in-law at Blackmore, there would be at least two more days of travel, most likely three, before they would reach the outskirts of Oban, especially along this terrain.

Unease settled into Garrick's bones. There was something he was missing. He knew that. His care for Brenna, losing what remained of his family and his own fatigue blocked his reason and logic. He cared for her too much, and the loss of Westmoreland, his family and his clan only clouded his judgement further. He cursed himself. He had to keep his distance physically and emotionally so he could protect her, but how could he do that? They were travelling together, pressed limb to limb, and the contact and memories it conjured within him were as pungent as they'd always been.

Always were too soft to be laird. Why God struck yer brother down and not ye, I'll ne'er understand.

The memory of his father's words after his brother's burial cut through Garrick deeply, for he feared the old man was right, as he had been about most matters with the clan. It was the other parts, of being a father and husband, that he hadn't quite got right.

Garrick couldn't afford to make any mistakes with Brenna. Her life depended on his decisions and the burden of that weighed upon him like slate in his veins.

Montgomerie skidded along the slick moss and small rocks, and Garrick shifted his weight to help offset the strain on his beloved stallion. Soon, they would need to dismount and walk, as the next section appeared more treacherous, especially in this weather, and far too dangerous for them to ride through even on a horse as experienced as his.

Brenna had not spoken a word since their escape from the man in the woods earlier in the morn. They rode on in an eerie silence. A silence that he found unsettling as the hours passed one after another. He frowned. The woman he'd known a year ago would have chatted away to avoid silence about the latest fashion, the exploits of her sister or whatever else she'd found of interest in the latest broadsheet. But this woman, this Brenna, he found he didn't know at all. He couldn't help but wonder what had happened while he'd been away.

She knew how to down a man with a blade, didn't hesitate to assist him in a fight and had agreed to marry an Englishman she didn't know for the sake of her clan and to please her father. The last year had changed them both, it seemed.

He batted away what role he'd played in such a change. Had his absence pushed her to this? To choose a future with a man she did not know to please a father who had never really respected her or her worth? While Garrick's regrets and guilt wouldn't keep her safe, his fierce resolve to protect her would. He would focus on that and that alone. He could grieve his family and recriminate himself for his mistakes later, but for now he would be present and alert. Getting Brenna to safety and discovering what had put her in harm's way in the first place was all that mattered.

As they reached the bottom of the ravine, he spied a small stream. It was a perfect spot to rest after such a long journey this morn. He narrowed his gaze and scanned the horizon. It was also an ideal area for an ambush, but they had been riding for hours, and a break would do them all good, especially with them both wounded. They needed to reach safety alive, and the best way to do that was to keep their wits about them by resting when they could and by taking a few minutes to look over what they'd found on the dead man. The turn in the road towards Glenhaven or Oban was ahead. A decision had to be made. And, once made, there would be no turning back. They had to be certain of their choice, as it might save or endanger their very lives.

'We'll stop here,' he said as they rounded a section of tall boulders.

Again, she said nothing in response.

He brought Montgomerie to a halt, dismounted and offered Brenna his hand. She slid her chilled petite hand into his, the sweet friction of her touch sending a gentle hum through his body. She avoided his gaze, hopped to the ground and let go of his hand.

'I'll return shortly,' she stated and began to walk off into the edge of the clearing behind a tree.

'Wait,' he commanded and jogged over to her. 'After what happened the last time, let me check the area first.'

Even though Brenna rolled her eyes at him, she paused, allowing him to pass. 'I *am* able to fend for myself. Perhaps you've noticed?' She crossed her arms against her chest.

'Aye. I have,' he called from behind her in the trees. 'I'm interested to know how you gained such skills since I've been away.' He emerged from the trees and set his gaze upon her.

Colour filled her cheeks and she walked past him, ignoring him entirely. 'One does what they have to when they have been abandoned.'

Her words cut him, no doubt as she had intended. He

kept his cursed response to himself. Squabbling with her would not help their cause, and if he was honest with himself she had reason to be angry. He had abandoned her by never sending word. In truth he had been a coward, but he was not quite strong enough to admit that to her out loud.

Brenna returned not long after and knelt by the stream to splash the cool water upon her face and take her fill of drink. He unpacked their saddlebags and knelt beside her, with a groan as his stitches pulled, to hand her more dried meat. As meagre as it was, it was far better than nothing.

She shook her head.

'You must eat. You'll not get far without sustenance. Eat. Please.'

Her gaze flicked up to him at the 'Please,' and a notch formed between her brows. 'How did you know that man would be carrying something hidden among his...?' She paused and gestured to his crotch.

It was his turn to blush. He cleared his throat. 'A soldier's hiding place. A necessary evil to protect what is most valuable to you.' He rose and scanned the area to ensure they were alone.

'That pouch you found was from Father. I am sure of it. I gave it to Stephen when I arrived in Oban to visit. The coin was an early dowry gift meant to hasten our union. Father was in quite the rush to secure the arrangement. He never said exactly why. I assumed it was due to his illness, but now I am uncertain. There may have been some other reason than the attack on your clan. One he did not see fit to share with me.'

'Such as?' Garrick asked, sitting down next to her with the saddlebag and strips of meat.

'At first glance, I could tell the packet of letters and correspondence had a variety of seals on them, but I didn't get a chance to take a good look. It's an odd thing for a stranger to have along with a pouch of coin, isn't it?'

'Not if they were a mercenary or hired soldier with a specific duty to fulfil. They may have been instructions and payment.'

She paled. 'Who would want to kill me?'

'I don't know.'

Garrick bit off a hunk of meat and then grabbed the stack of bound letters from the saddlebag. He tugged the ribbon off and split the stack in two, placing another strip of dried meat on the pile before handing it to her. 'You take half, and I'll take the other. Perhaps when we share what we have each found we'll have a clearer idea of what is afoot.'

She took the letters as well as the meat, nibbling off smaller bits as she opened each letter and read the contents. Garrick opened the top one of his stack of correspondence and read with interest.

Dear Sir,
Time is of the essence as we finalise our merger.
The coin we require is past due. You will need to
secure your position by sending us proof of your
commitment to the cause.
M

He frowned. Vague, odd and not of great use, Garrick set it down and continued to the next letter. The contents sent a chill through his bones.

Dear M,
My interest is sound and payment will come to
you as soon as I am wed. I am sending proof of
my commitment until the rest has been secured.
SW

'What did you say this Mr Winters' business interests were? Shipping?'

Brenna shrugged. 'And assorted investments.' She nibbled on another piece of meat and continued reading from a letter.

Garrick picked up the next one and the dread he had been feeling in his gut only increased. By the time he'd finished his stack, the dried meat tasted like ash in his mouth, but he swallowed it down anyway.

Brenna finished the last of her stack and met his gaze. 'All business letters. Yours?'

'The same. Who are the letters from and to?'

She frowned. 'Although I cannot be absolutely certain, it appears to be a series of letters back and forth from my Mr Winters, Father and some other person signed off as "M."'

'Mine as well. When were yours dated? This stack is very recent. Within the last month.'

'These are older, dating back to the beginning of talks of my engagement three months ago.' Her gaze dropped away and a bitter laugh fell from her lips.

'Father was in talks about this engagement well before mentioning it to me. Made me believe it was my choice, and I thought I was doing something to please him and make him proud of me by choosing to marry Mr Winters for the sake of the clan.'

She handed Garrick the letters, her fingertips skimming his palm. 'I was a fool. He had set our marriage in motion before I even knew of the possibility of it. He set the stage and I played into it as a fine, yet unwilling, actor.'

Sadness pulled down the corners of her eyes when she met his gaze. What could he say to that? This was not the first time Bran had used his daughters as pawns in a game of gaining more power for his clan in the Highlands. He'd done the same with her older sister Moira, with rather dire consequences. Garrick wasn't shocked at the revelation, but such words would not lessen the blow to Brenna. Despite all, she loved her father, and had always sought his love and approval.

A gift the man seemed incapable of giving her.

He swallowed hard. It was a gift Garrick had stolen from her as well by wilfully abandoning her. Did that make him as horrid as her father? He wouldn't allow himself the time to puzzle through to an answer. He needed to manage one crisis at a time.

He resisted the urge to reach out to comfort her. 'You are no fool. Just a daughter in search of approval from her father. I did the same with my own. Became a soldier to please him. I believed it would help him see my worth.'

She met his gaze. 'You never told me such. Did it work?'

'Nay. Hamish MacLean was always more impressed by my eldest brother, Lon. While I was jealous of Lon for the love and praise he earned from my father, I never resented him. He was a great man. He would have been a fine laird if the fever had not claimed him. Father never recovered from his loss. He rather resented it wasn't me or Cairn who perished, and we found it hard to compete with my eldest brother's memories. In the end, we gave up our efforts and focused our care on Mother. When Father died, we found we had already grieved him long ago.'

'How long did that take?'

'I'll let you know.' Garrick smiled at her. 'Give yourself credit, Brenna. You are a fine, talented woman. This Stephen Winters is lucky to have you for a wife. My hope is that he endeavours to deserve you, no matter what ideas your father has put in your head about your worth.'

Brenna edged away from him, wiping a tear from her cheek before tucking her legs under her. He forged ahead with his findings and swallowed back the tight ache at the base of his throat. He knew the hurt she felt, and no further words from him would change it. No gentle touch from him would make it better either, but merely make it worse for them both. He'd focus on her safety instead.

'Was he supposed to accompany you back to Glenhaven?' he asked.

'You mean Stephen?'

He nodded.

'Aye. He was. He was even packed and had planned to stay a day or two at Glenhaven, but he received a note by messenger before we were to set out. He went to his study with the man and then, when he emerged again, he said it was imperative he stay and sort out an issue with a shipment that had arrived early at the docks.'

Garrick stilled. 'That makes little sense. Why not simply delay your departure a day?'

'I was in a hurry to return to Glenhaven. I was rather bored, and with Father so ill I thought it best. When Arthur and his son offered to transport me home, I eagerly accepted.'

'And Winters allowed it?'

'Without hesitation. I thought nothing of it at the time but, now that I think upon it, he was behaving strangely. He was rather preoccupied when I left. He sent the messenger out to the docks with a package. Now, I am wondering what exactly was in it.'

'Could it have been the pouch?'

'It was larger than the pouch. About the size of a milliner's box.'

Her comparison made him smile. She had always loved hats. He could remember taking her to the milliner's shop in Edinburgh more than once over the months of their courtship.

'I've been puzzling over it all this morning. Why would he have Father's pouch? Was it his or for delivery to someone else? Did he steal it, or did Stephen give it to him? And why? Did he owe them coin and he was repaying a debt? And what's the importance in all of those letters?'

'All fine questions.' Garrick chewed upon the meat, although he couldn't really taste it. His gut was plaguing him. He couldn't resolve what she had told him in his mind. They were missing something.

'How did your father even come to meet this Mr Winters?' Garrick asked.

She shrugged. She'd either ignored or hadn't noticed the edge in his voice regarding her fiancé. 'Father met him through an acquaintance of the King.'

He balked. 'Why was he meeting with the King? I've never known your father to want to spend any time with the man.'

'It was not by choice, I assure you. Fear made him do it, and Father does not fear much, as you well know.'

Garrick studied her as she braided her hair into a long dark plait and tried to comb out the tangles with her fingers. Despite how focused her hands were upon such a task, she stared out at the stream unseeing, her thoughts consumed elsewhere.

His gut tightened again. She was omitting something by choice, but what?

'You didn't ask for more information about this man you were to marry?'

She tied off a ribbon at the end of her hair and set a glare upon him. 'Of course I did. I'm not daft. I want to know about my future. I am not merely a decoration.' Her words were sharp, tiny splinters sent his way. They hit their mark with ease, and he felt like a bastard.

'You know you are far more than that. I wasn't implying…' he began, attempting to soften the cut his words had made.

'Weren't you?'

'What has happened to make you believe I think so little of you?'

She met his gaze and the hurt in her eyes stole his breath. He had his answer. He'd abandoned her. Left her to believe he was dead.

Aye. He'd been a selfish bastard.

She didn't need to say it for him to know it. He cleared his throat and swallowed the emotion knotted up there. The wind whipped along the hillside and he turned his body away from it, only to see clouds rolling in off in the distance. 'Looks like rain will be moving in well before nightfall. Best we hurry. If you agree, I think it is safer to travel to Blackmore. If these men were intentionally tracking you or your father, they will go to Glenhaven next. It is a more obvious choice.'

'Will Father and Ewan be in danger?' Brenna asked, alarm lifting the pitch of her words.

'Nay. They would not go to the estate outright. Most likely they would wait for you along the road and intercept you there. Make it look like a band of thieves.'

'Like last time,' she mumbled quietly.

'Aye. I am quite certain those men were hired to track you, and either capture or kill you, but I am not certain by whom or why.'

Although, he feared it might be her beloved fiancé. The dead man had Winters' coin in his pocket with correspondence between Bran, himself and some other man. The real question was, who had given it to him with the order to attack? Had it been Winters, 'M,' or another man that Winters had paid? Either way, he didn't trust this fiancé of hers, not a whit. The man was involved somehow, or daft as driftwood. Neither was good enough for Brenna.

Although the need to continue their travels to avoid the weather had spared him from having to discuss the horrid possibilities of who was behind the initial attack on her, as well as her anger at him, Garrick knew they'd have to talk eventually. They needed to work together to get to Oban safely and they couldn't do that while keeping a bevy of secrets between them.

But he wanted to do that as much as he'd like to walk across a field of thistles with bare feet covered in open sores. He'd avoid it as long as he could. She would think him jaded to imply Winters was behind the attack, which would lead to them discussing their own past. He clenched his jaw.

'Best we walk alongside Montgomerie for this next pass. It's quite narrow and steep.'

'As you wish,' she muttered, the edge in her voice unmistakable.

Perhaps he should have been grateful for the previous silence.

They plodded along at a steady pace. The temperature dropped sharply as they neared the edge of the cliffside. Garrick watched for sites to serve as possible shelter as they went up and down hill after hill, the sun lowering at every turn. When he saw an abandoned shell of a church as an early dusk clawed along the horizon, he groaned, but decided it was the best protection they had for the night. The irony was not lost on him. Ayleen would have had a grand chuckle, seeing him walk across the threshold of a holy place so soon after promising he never would again.

'We'll stay here for the night,' he grumbled, leading them through the waist-high crumbling rock wall surrounding the old, abandoned building. The sight of it sent a shiver along his spine. He hadn't been in a church since the night he'd lost Ayleen. The crucifix he wore felt like ice against his throat. He pinched the bridge of his nose to push back the memories of that night.

Focus on Brenna.

He released a breath and rolled his neck. He was weary and his side and arm ached. He settled Montgomerie in the courtyard shaded by a large tree that had grown through the dilapidated remnants of the roof and came back to Brenna. She sat on the rock wall, gazing out at the sea.

'A rainbow,' she murmured. 'Just past the break in the cliffs to the west.'

He followed her hand, the petite fingers looking as if they were dancing upon the array of pastels that arched across the sky. It looked more to him like a sunset than a rainbow, but he smiled just the same. If it gave her a moment of pleasure, he wished for it to be a smattering of rainbows.

He frowned. He was being a fool. He shook his head and turned away. His stitches pulled and he winced. 'We need to change your dressings,' she stated, glancing at his side.

The last thing he wanted was to be fussed over,

but he knew she was right. Otherwise, he might get an infection and slow their journey to Oban, or leave her exposed to attack, which would be even worse. He shrugged, which was as close to an agreement as he could muster.

'I'll take that as a yes,' she answered and patted the rock wall next to her.

He sat down with a thump and pulled up the side of his tunic.

'I'll get your kit,' she said and returned. She pulled out what she needed and set them out on the ledge.

As she unwrapped the makeshift bandages, he winced and then focused his attention out to the sea. The more he stared out, the more he began to see that rainbow.

Bloody rainbow.

He needed a plan, not hope. It was just like God to send him a rainbow rather than a fellow soldier with reinforcements to protect them. A rainbow would help him as much as a bucket of rotten fish.

Brenna cleaned his wound without a word. She rinsed it with water and covered it with salve from his kit, which numbed some of the pain. He closed his eyes in relief. He hadn't realised how much it had been plaguing him as he'd ridden until the throbbing began to fade.

'Whose crucifix is that?' Brenna whispered. The words set his heart thundering and his eyes shot open.

'Ayleen's.'

Her touch softened as she continued to wrap his side with care with a new strip of linen torn from her underskirts. Saying Ayleen's name made his throat ache. Regret burned like acid as he swallowed down the memories.

'What happened to her? To you?' She smoothed the last wrap around his side and tucked an edge gently under it to keep it in place.

Her blue eyes settled on him like the summer sky, and he faltered. She was another beacon of hope that God kept sending him, and it became harder to bat her away, even if it was for her own good. When she was here beside him, all warm, soft, kind and comforting, all he wanted was to touch her.

He dropped his gaze from her and reached for his tunic.

She was meant for another man. Not him. He had never deserved her, especially not now.

'I didn't get there in time. It's as simple as that. I failed her. I failed all of them.'

Before Brenna could say a word, Garrick rose from the wall and shrugged on his tunic and coat with a wince. 'I'll find some wood for the fire. Stay here.'

She opened her mouth but then closed it. She knew *this* Garrick. The man who ran from the past and pushed himself through pain. Pain so deep it had no bottom, no end. Part of her knew she couldn't bring him back from it—not alone, anyway. He'd have to want to come back to her and she wasn't sure he wanted to. And, with all that had happened between them, she wasn't sure she did either. He had chosen to allow her to believe he was dead.

His silhouette cut into the night sky behind him, obliterating the stars in his path. Her body still sung at the sight of him, just as it had that cool autumn day years ago when they'd first met at Glenhaven at the tournament of champions—the yearly assemblage of lairds and their first sons to show their strength and prowess. A man of duty, strength, and honour. She'd never met a man like Garrick before or a man of his equal since.

He disappeared from view, and the familiar loss began as a slight tingling in her fingertips. He'd been gone for over a year, and she had worked hard, very hard, to forget him, grieve him. She'd almost succeeded.

She frowned at the realisation that she couldn't let go all of him and the hope she had had for their future. She still clung to some tiny gossamer thread of hope for them, which was ridiculous. He didn't want her. He'd made that as clear as the summer sky. And she was engaged to another man.

She was being a fool to let his reappearance change any plans she'd already set in motion, wasn't she? She'd grieved him and accepted her fate as part of an arranged marriage proposed by Father to provide their clan protection as the tensions in the country grew. But now, knowing that Garrick was alive and that Father had all but manipulated her into this arrangement, she hesitated. Could she embrace a marriage and a future without love, knowing Garrick was alive? Could they even try to love one another again after all that had happened between them?

She didn't know.

He had deceived her, just like her father.

He'd allowed her to believe one thing while he'd made a decision about her future without her consent. Why had he done it? Did he not believe her capable of making her own decisions?

Garrick came back into view carrying a load of wood and tinder. A slight hitch in his step and grimace along his brow were the only signs of his injury, but she knew he was hurting. The man she had once loved, still loved, was buried under that shell of wounds and guilt over the agony of the past. She approached him to offer to carry some of the weight. To her surprise, he allowed it, and his fingers feathered along her own lightly, accidentally. She clutched the dead branches and twigs to her chest.

'Is it safe to start a fire? Will we be seen?' she rushed out. The confusion over her feelings for him and the tremble of awareness his touch had stirred in her made her words trip over themselves.

His hands faltered as he arranged the tinder along the dead branches of the fire he was building. He shrugged. 'It's a risk, but a storm is coming. I can feel it in my shoulder. It aches before the first snow. And based on that...' he paused, setting the last of the tinder beneath it '...there'll be snow in the morning. We may freeze without the warmth of the fire.'

She shuddered involuntarily and rubbed her arms. Snow would only hamper their progress and make the journey that much more treacherous and uncomfortable. They had scarce enough clothing and food between them to manage to Oban as it was, which was at least two more days out. And her blasted slippers. Her toes might freeze and snap off if she had to walk in the snow for that long.

Garrick walked over to her, removed his coat and draped it around her, his palms skimming the round, soft slope of her shoulders. 'We'll make it. I promise.' The intensity and certainty of his words made her eyes tear up, and she was grateful he couldn't see her blink them back. How did he always know what she was thinking and exactly what she needed to hear?

The warmth of his coat, and knowing it had come from his body, made her shiver once more and he rubbed her arms. She didn't want to give it up, but he was wounded and, despite everything, she still cared for him, even if he had been cruel by staying away.

'Nay,' she said, clearing her throat and thrusting herself back to the present. 'I can't take your coat. You'll freeze.'

He chuckled. 'That's why I'm building the fire.'

'How are we going to make it all the way to Oban in the snow without help? You're wounded. You need to rest before you collapse.'

His cheeks had lost colour since yesterday, and the pinched expression in his face grown more distinct. He was pretending all was fine, as everyone always did around her, as if she were a fragile dandelion that might lose all of its petals if a strong wind came. She wasn't her sister Moira, but she could withstand a great deal more than her family gave her credit for. She picked up some kindling and handed it to him, awaiting an answer.

'I don't need you to fuss over me,' he grumbled, shaking his head.

She lifted her chin. He'd retreated once more. 'Maybe you do, Garrick. Have you not ever thought upon that? We're stuck with one another until Oban. You might as well let me help keep *you* alive. We need each other, no matter how you may feel about it.'

He squatted by the fire, which was beginning to wink with life. They both watched the flickering flames come alive. She grabbed a tartan from Montgomerie and spread it out before the fire. The warmth was as delicious as the coat still wrapped around her shoulders. She sat down, crossing her legs so her feet were close to the fire, and put her chilled hands palms out. She sighed as the warmth began to seep into her hands and frozen toes.

Garrick rose and joined her on the tartan. They sat in silence, watching the fire continue to burn, sending smoke into the midnight-blue sky. Clouds were coming in slowly, blocking out patches of stars and soon the moon.

One thing he was right about. A storm was coming.

Chapter Seven

Brenna's logic was sound. Garrick knew in his mind that they needed to work together to survive. He was injured, as was she, and the weather would hamper their journey, but his heart hated the idea. He didn't want her to need him, as that left room for him to fail her as he had already failed everyone else he loved.

He swallowed hard as the flames curled up and down the dry tinder, casting shadows along the crumbling walls and half-exposed ceiling of the abandoned church. He hated the dark. It always had a way of letting in the past. No matter how hard he tried to keep the reality away, he couldn't.

They were dead. They were all dead. Because of him. Hot tears burned the back of his eyes and his throat constricted. His sister, Ayleen. His younger brother, Cairn. His beautiful mother. And here he'd thought losing his father and eldest brother were the only losses he would have to bear! What an arrogant fool he had been to stay away. And being here with

Brenna, the one woman who had softened the sharp edges of the world into something smoother, more beautiful and manageable, was promised to another?

Saints be. How much could a man take? Especially when he knew he had caused it by staying away. And now he wasn't even sure he was strong enough to protect her.

He blinked back the tears that threatened and cleared his throat to loosen the cry of anguish that hung there waiting to be released. It couldn't be today, nor tomorrow. He had to be clear and alert, not clouded by heartbreak. And, besides, his tears wouldn't change anything. Nothing would bring them back. Hope was a belief for foolish men, and he wouldn't be one of them. Not this time.

The twig he had been holding snapped in two in his hand, forcing him back to the present. He turned his head, only to find Brenna staring at him. The concern and care in her gaze irritated him, so he turned away, ignoring her unspoken questions. If she'd truly loved him, she would have waited. But she hadn't, and he couldn't forgive her for it. Or himself, for daring to let her go.

They'd both been fools.

He tossed the two tiny twigs into the fire and savoured the snap and crackle as they were eaten away by the flames. Nature, he understood. The elements, he understood. People and the ways of life, he didn't. If he'd only left a day earlier or later, he wouldn't have encountered Brenna at all. He would have returned and found her promised to another. He would have grieved, but he could have avoided her until the wound had healed.

He stilled. But she'd also be dead if he'd not come along when he had. No one would have found her before the men doubled back to kill her. He shivered. He would never have wished that, never, but by all that was holy why did it have to be him to have found her and be charged with keeping her safe?

'My mother died on a night like this. Cool, haunting and full of stars.'

Brenna's words were so soft, so light, Garrick wondered if he'd imagined them. He turned to her. She continued staring far off into the distance through the large gaping hole in the battered stone wall before them.

'One moment she was alive, laughing and full of joy, and the next she was gone. Some limp, lifeless creature on the floor I did not recognise. Everyone else reacted, did something, anything, but I just stared. I could not reconcile that it was her. I kept waiting for her to wake, but she never did. It was the only time I'd ever seen Father cry. And I was so unnerved by it that I sat staring at him. Moira offered him comfort, so did Ewan. But me?' She shrugged. 'I sat on the floor next to Mother's still form, running her hair through my fingertips. Praying that life from my touch would flow into her like fairy magic.' She shook her head. 'Ridiculous, I know.'

'Nay. No more so than me wearing this cross of Ayleen's, wishing it might bring her back to me.' He met her gaze and then looked at her hand. 'But it does explain why you rub the ends of your hair between your fingers when you are restless or worried.'

Her brow furrowed and she let go of the end of the plait of hair that she had been absently running her fingertips through. 'Do I do that?'

He smiled at her. 'Aye. I always found it endearing, even more so now that I know the cause.'

Colour rose in her cheeks and she looked away. 'I still miss her. And I wonder about all of the things she would have taught me and what advice she would have given me, especially about Father.'

'Oh?' Garrick asked.

'He is a difficult man, as you well know, but even more so now that he has been so ill and not himself. She always knew how to calm him, settle him, when he was angry or agitated.'

Garrick sat up and moved closer to her, his hand resting on her forearm. 'When did this happen, these changes in him?'

She pulled the coat around her more tightly, causing his hand to fall away. 'Six months past, perhaps a bit more. The doctor says it is his heart, but I wonder if it has affected his logic. When I think about how this arrangement came to be and those letters, it is nonsensical. I'm sorry. I am blathering on.'

'Nay. All we have now is time and the cold. Talking may help the time pass and the cold lessen. It may also help us figure out what is truly going on.'

Brenna clenched her teeth. *Ack.* Why did he have to be so kind? His kindness could be a weapon if used well, as it was now. She shifted and continued on in hopes it would distract her from the biting winds.

'Father tires easily and sleeps much more than he used to. He had quite a serious episode several months ago, and he has never quite recovered. He is determined to have all of his affairs in order and Ewan and I settled before he passes. Men of the clan roam in and out of Glenhaven at all hours with his orders. Since all that happened with your family, he is driven to secure our clan's status within the King's eyes as well, no matter the cost. It is why he is so desperate to finalise my match with Mr Winters, despite hardly knowing the man at all.'

She didn't dare snatch a glimpse of Garrick. Nor did she need to. She could feel the heat of his displeasure on her as if his gaze was the sun. Moments ticked by before he responded.

'How does he know such a match will secure anything for him? Assurances and alliances are far from certain. Those along the Borderlands can attest to that.' He threw another small twig he'd found on the ground into the fire.

'He is certain, despite no further assurances other than the man's word. And, in my haste to bring him peace, I agreed. I did not know he already had made the agreement. My word didn't matter a whit.'

Perhaps I am as useless as Father said.

She batted away the thought.

'And Ewan and Moira have agreed to such a union?'

She shifted and brought the coat collar up to cover her ears. 'Neither of them has any say against Father, and as I said, Moira does not even know of it. I did not wish to tell her until it was finalised.'

'I cannot wait to see her reaction when she finds out.'

Brenna squared her shoulders, a flare of jealousy budding within her. Garrick respected Moira, and they had always had some silent understanding between them since they'd met at the Tournament of Champions years ago, one that she could never quite get to the bottom of. Of course, she'd also never asked either of them. Directness was not one of her strengths. She fiddled with the end of her plait and then batted it away once she realised she was doing it. She glanced up to see him smirking at her.

'What?' she asked.

'Why did you not tell her? Plead for her help or interference? She knows first-hand the ill effects of your father's matches. She would have come to your aid, and so would Rory. They would have assisted you without question.'

Garrick was right. Moira did understand. She had scarce survived her first husband, a match made by Father. Peter Fraser had been cruel in the worst ways a man could be, and she'd suffered in silence until his death. Rory was the husband she had deserved the first time around, despite Brenna's own initial reservations about her sister marrying him.

But that would not be her fate. Stephen Winters didn't seem a cruel man, merely a disinterested and arrogant fiancé, and there were worse things than that, weren't there?

'Because I could not bear to,' she muttered. 'I am trying desperately to make my own way and to not be quite so cast under her shadow.'

'What?' Garrick asked. 'What on earth are you talking about—her shadow?'

'I—I cannot make you understand,' she faltered, fiddling with the end of his coat sleeve instead of her hair. 'You are…*you*.'

'Aye. Is that bad?' he asked.

'Nay, but it makes you completely unable to see my position on the matter.' She lifted her chin.

'How so?'

'You are a laird. A soldier lauded for your achievements on the field, respected for your rank and skill. You are a man who does not doubt himself. You do not know what it feels like to be the one that has no impact on the world. If I disappeared or blew away in the wind tomorrow, it would not matter. I have made no claim, no imprint. No one would even notice my absence.' She hated the quiver of desperation she heard in her voice, but it was the truth. Being nothing scared her far more than being married to an Englishman she did not know.

He studied her. A war waged in his moss-green eyes. She didn't know what it was about, but she could see it. Finally, he nodded. 'I do understand that. More than you know.'

She scoffed at him. 'I doubt it.'

The mask fell back in place, and before her eyes the emotion in him disappeared like an animal hiding in a forest. He shifted away from her and closer to the fire.

A pit opened in her stomach. Perhaps he did know,

but she'd batted his attempt to connect with her aside like a pesky fly.

Blast.

'Garrick, I did not mean to…'

He didn't answer but gestured behind her to the saddlebags. 'Can you gather the letters and pouch we found this morning on the man who attacked you? Reading through them again may help us get to the heart of why those men were after you and how we can ensure your safe return back to Oban.'

She let the matter go and turned to gather the items from the bag. Why was she always mucking up the important bits? He'd almost opened up to her, which she knew was hard for him, but she'd truly thought he was joking and had batted his statement away. She never imagined he would understand how small and insignificant she felt at times. Why would he ever doubt his self-worth, with all he had achieved in his life?

Now she'd never know. Garrick had receded back into his armour of safety like a turtle into its shell. Who knew when he would feel safe enough to try again, if ever?

She handed him the items, letting her fingertips linger along his hand. 'I'm sorry,' she murmured, attempting to build a bridge of words back to the moment that had been severed between them.

He stilled and then pulled his hand away. 'No matter,' he answered and set to the task at hand. Just like Garrick—always focused, logical, neutral. Emotion rarely clouded his judgement.

Reason always ruled.

It was enough to make a woman go mad.

She knew the moment he reached the end of the notes she had read, which held her father's signature, as his neutral mask fell into a scowl.

'This is from your father,' he stated, as if that was new information to them both rather than just her.

'I know.'

'Care to share how and why that man would have had it?' Garrick frowned at her.

She raised her hands in confusion. 'I do not know why he has it. I believe it was the same note, paired with the coin that I brought from Glenhaven and gave to Mr Winters, that ensured our marriage was secured to move forward, as it was a fresh deal. Or at least that is what Father said. That terms had been agreed to, but it could be an older letter. I could be wrong. I don't know why these men would have it. Perhaps he was repaying a debt to them, and the note was included to show the marriage was official, and more coin would be coming their way for whatever endeavour he was working towards?'

'That would explain the coin, but not why they would have the note. It is an invitation for him to visit Glenhaven upon your return. No mercenary would need such a note.'

'Mr Winters does seem rather distractable. Maybe he gave him them both in error?'

Garrick gifted her a droll look and she flushed. 'I know. It sounds ridiculous, but I can think of no other reason why that stranger would have had it and gone to such measures to secure it…hide it…as he did. And then to track me, Arthur and Roland down, only to try to kill us.'

'Did you meet anyone there on your visit? Walk in on a conversation or meeting you shouldn't have?'

She paused and recollected her days at Winters' estate. 'I cannot recall anything of that nature. I spent more time with his household staff than him. In fact, I got to know Arthur and Roland rather well. They were both very kind to me.'

Garrick scrubbed a hand through his hair as he stared into the fire. 'I have an idea, but it also makes little sense. Unless there is a more complex reason at play.'

A gust of wind made her shiver. 'And that is?' Brenna enquired, shifting closer to him.

'Has Mr Winters ever visited Glenhaven before?'

She paused. 'Nay. We have always travelled to him. He does not enjoy the Highlands. Something about it being too cold.'

'Sounds like a real prize,' Garrick muttered under his breath.

She rolled her eyes. 'You were saying possible reasons?'

He continued. 'He may have brought it with him to gain quick entrance at Glenhaven if needed. The man could have merely shown the letter with its seal to the guards at the door, given the name of Stephen Winters and been admitted without question, since he is your betrothed.'

Her heart thudded against her chest. 'Aye,' she replied. 'I suppose.' She bit her lip. 'Only Father has met him, other than the soldiers who escorted me there this time. He sends the same few trusted men with me during each excursion to ensure my safety.' She paused. 'And…they are still gathering supplies and have not yet returned home, so the servants would have no idea if the man was Mr Winters or not, and allowed him in.' Nerves chewed along her skin. 'Garrick, no one would have been aware. Ewan wouldn't even know. But why would the man bother with such a ruse if Father would know immediately of the deceit upon seeing him?'

Garrick paused and pressed his lips together.

'Tell me why,' she pleaded.

He faced her and his grim features warned her that she wouldn't like his answer. Not one bit. 'It wouldn't matter if your goal was to kill the man you met with.'

She recoiled. 'You can't mean that. Why would Stephen… Mr Winters…or anyone send men to kill Father?'

'It would be a great way to incite a maelstrom of discontent and sew more discord and unrest in the Highlands, which would then require the King's men to come and subdue us. It may not have mattered which clan leader, but merely a prominent one. And Bran fits that requirement.'

She gasped. 'What if there are others? How can we get word to Father and Ewan?'

'There may be others, but I don't believe they will be able to gain entry without these items before the Stewart soldiers return with supplies. And, even if we could send word from here, it would not reach Glenhaven in time. We must trust that stopping this one man will keep them safe.'

For now.

It was little comfort. She clutched her hands together in worry.

'What are your terms in the marriage contract?'

Her mind raced and she hid her face in her hands. 'I didn't ask,' she grumbled.

She cursed herself. Why didn't she ask? Why had she trusted these men with her future and not enquired?

Garrick caressed her head, and it lingered down to the nape of her neck, sending a trill of awareness through her. 'Brenna?'

'Aye,' she answered. Heat flushed her body. Had she been a fool once more? Had her lack of involvement left her father and brother at risk?

Useless.

'Look at me,' he urged, rubbing her shoulder.

She forced herself to drop her hands, much as she didn't wish to. The last thing she wanted was to be shamed once more for her mistakes, but she saw no judgement in his eyes.

'It does not matter. If this man was eager to dispense with your Father, or at least gain entry into Glenhaven without detection, he would have found whatever means of entry he needed. This may have just been the avenue they chose to take. And we don't even know if that was the reason. As you know, I am jaded and a sceptic. The past has made me that way. I could be wrong on all counts. We both could be.'

'What I fear is that you are right. Your judgement is sound...' She paused, unable to keep the next words from falling from her lips. 'About most things.'

He stilled and removed his hand, as if he'd only realised he was consoling her, and her barb had added impact.

Old patterns were so easy to fall into. She could physically drop back into being comforted and cared for by Garrick as easily as she'd shrugged on his coat, but the past had severed her emotional trust in him and shredded it into ribbons. Her heart couldn't forget or forgive him for showing her a future as bright as a sea of rainbows, only to leave her empty-handed and out in the blinding rain, unable to see but an arm's length ahead of her.

Chapter Eight

Garrick woke with a shiver. Despite being partially protected by what was left of the roof of the abandoned church, he was covered in a light dusting of snow. Brenna was snuggled against him, and his body had curved around her limbs in a protective and unconscious shell. Only small flakes had settled in her hair and along the slope of her back. He should move. *Now.* She was engaged to another. His body ignored his mind's command, so he studied her, memorised her features for later, when all he could do was dream of her and remember this moment when she was tucked in against him.

The imperfect curve of the tiny lashes along her closed eyes fluttered and her slightly parted lips moved. She was dreaming. Of him? Probably not. Even the nasty bluish purple gash along her temple veiled in black wavy hair was beautiful. She could have been his. She *had* been his. As he had been hers. His body trembled, knowing full well what it had lost, what he had consciously given away: his happiness.

But when he'd heard of the reivers rushing along the Borderlands, knowing full well that Ayleen's abbey was along its path, all he'd been able to think of was going and rescuing her. And then he'd arrived and, when he'd had the moment to protect her, he'd frozen. He'd watched his baby sister die at the hands of raiders who cared nothing for her kind heart and generous soul. The memory of her hand reaching for him as the life emptied from her eyes was as clear and terrifying as it had been the moment it'd happened.

He swallowed hard and shuddered, snow tumbling off him. Her death and the death of his family were a reminder of why Brenna was best without him. When it counted, he hadn't been able to protect them. While he was effective on the battlefield, when it came to matters of those he loved, he fell short. He froze and wasn't there for them.

So far, he'd been lucky in being able to keep Brenna safe and alive, but each moment when she'd been thrust in danger his heart had stopped, the dread of past losses hot along his skin. And if he ran out of luck…it would cost her life.

Carefully, he separated his interwoven limbs from hers and brushed the snow from his clothes. He thought about doing the same for Brenna, but that would require touching her, which seemed a poor idea. He fisted his hands at his sides, stepped outside the remnants of the church walls and watched the sun struggling to pull its weight up into the sky.

He knew exactly how he felt. Tired.

His body ached and he was growing weaker. The

lack of food, demanding journey and blood loss would continue to take its toll. But they'd need to travel at least two more days, and the snowfall might make it three. He scrubbed his hand down his face. How in the world would they make it three more days out here with such meagre supplies and enemies possibly still giving chase?

He frowned. They wouldn't. Another opportunity would present itself or he'd make one. That was their only viable option.

'How did you sleep?' Brenna asked. He turned to see her covering her mouth as she yawned. She was sitting up in front of the remnants of the fire that had long since gone out.

'Like the dead again, which might have got us killed.' He had fought off sleep for as long as he could last night, but fatigue had claimed him. He'd used more luck he didn't have.

She frowned at him. '"Quite well" would have been an acceptable answer.'

He shrugged. 'Just being honest.'

'Sorry I asked,' she muttered and shifted to standing. She brushed off the snow.

'Do you need to…?' he asked, pointing to the woods.

'Aye,' she answered and headed towards him. Her skirts were a bedraggled mess of dirt and fabric, and she dragged them behind her. He hit his palm to his forehead. Why had he not thought of it sooner?

He rushed to the saddlebags, where he had an extra tunic and trews rolled up, and returned to her. 'Change,' he ordered, extending them to her.

She glanced down at the clothes and back at him. 'What?'

'Change into these. The men are following a man and a woman in a blue dress. If we both appear to be men from a distance, our chance of survival will improve tenfold. I forgot I even had them.'

'Any chance you have boots in there as well?' She pointed to her thin slippers.

He frowned. 'Nay.'

'Worth asking. These should be a might warmer and drier. Thank you.' She accepted the clothes and clutched them to her chest. He followed her to the woods at a distance.

'Turn,' she commanded, lifting an eyebrow.

He lifted his hands. 'Only trying to ensure your safety.' He turned and quirked a smile. He did wish to look. She had always had a fine form, but she was his no longer.

The idea would take a while to get used to.

Minutes later she returned, having finished her ablutions and changed into his spare clothes. His body heated as she drew closer. She seemed more naked than ever before. His thin tunic revealed the exquisite shape of her breasts and her tiny waist, as she had tucked it into his trews. Despite being far too large, his clothes gave him a clear idea of her shape. His throat dried.

'What's happened to your…erm…?' He gestured to her chest area.

'Corset?' she asked, holding up his trews, far too large for her, with one hand.

'Aye.' He cleared his throat. 'You seem…' Again he gestured to her breasts.

'Comfortable? Able to breathe?' She popped a hand to her hip and the sway of her breasts threatened to strike him dumb. 'Are those the words you are looking for?'

He didn't move. There seemed a right and wrong answer, and he didn't wish to choose the wrong one, so he shrugged, before adding in a final word. 'Liberated?'

She smiled. 'Aye. My breasts have been liberated so that, if I need to run from an attacker, I can take a full breath, so I don't pass out. Have you an extra belt or length of rope, by chance?'

'I can use a rope for your belt.' He grabbed a section of rope from his saddlebags and cut a strip. He started to tie it over her trews, so she could roll it over and secure the material in place, but thought better of it. Being too close wasn't good for his focus. She still affected him. Deeply. He handed her the length of rope that remained and stepped back as she cinched it around her waist. She rolled the excess material and tucked it in place. He draped the plaid back over her shoulders and secured it around as much of her body as he could to block the wind and to obscure her figure.

'Best we get moving before another round of snow comes upon us. You'll ride while I walk. And, if you see anyone or any livestock, tell me. We need to find food for us and Montgomerie.'

'How are we going to pay for it if we do find it? We could use Father's coin.'

'Nay. We'll barter. The coin will only draw more unwanted attention.' He packed up their meagre belongings and helped her to mount.

'What can we barter with?' she asked.

'With whatever we can. Our possessions will matter little if we're both dead.'

Garrick never had been one to mince words. But he was right. Her possessions wouldn't matter if she was dead, so there was no need to worry over what they would trade if they encountered anyone along their journey. Staying alive was the goal. She wouldn't be of much worth to her father, her family or the clan if she were dead. And, deep down, she wanted desperately to live and find a purpose greater than being a bargaining chip or game piece to be manoeuvred by the men in her life.

She just wasn't entirely sure how to go about it. She'd never been terribly good at anything except being pretty. She had dabbled in learning of herbs, as well as sewing, but she wasn't terribly good at either. The fact that she had thrown that blade and downed a man had surprised her as much as it had Garrick.

They set off south once more, taking extra care as they traversed up, down and through narrow passages. Some sections were enclosed on each side with large rocks and boulders worn smooth by the wind and rain, while others were precariously close to the cliff's edge. The waves crashed against the shoreline as the wind blew what was left of the light snow around them. The sound was a heady reminder of the sizeable drop it would be if Montgomerie lost his footing. Even with Garrick guiding the fine stallion by the reins as he walked alongside, Brenna still sat rigid and held her breath.

'Must we travel so close to the edge?' she asked, a quiver evident in her voice.

'Aye,' he answered, continuing. 'There is no other trail until we cut back through this section and join a path that runs parallel to the road.'

Montgomerie slipped on a stone and a few loose pebbles skidded off the side, disappearing into the water below.

'Curses,' she murmured.

He glanced back at her. 'Do we need to stop? Are you unwell?'

'Nay, nay. 'tis just the height. Keep going,' she urged. 'The last thing I want to do is stop at the cliff side. Just get us through this pass. As quickly and safely as possible.'

'Aye,' he answered. 'I had forgotten. Hold fast. We'll be through quickly.'

Brenna clutched at the reins and forced herself to breathe in and then out. She would be fine. Heights still bothered her no matter how she tried to move past it. The memory of almost falling to her death when she'd been but a wee lass was still as clear as if it had happened yesterday.

'Take my hand,' Ewan pleaded over the loud crashing of the waves below. The spray of the waves hit her

calves, and she clung to the roots on the ledge she had fallen to.

She looked down and shrieked. It was a long, long fall into the cold waters of the sea.

'Bren,' he said firmly, his voice confident and certain. 'Hold on to the root with one hand while reaching up to take mine with the other.'

'I don't know if I can!' she cried as she studied the distance between his hand and her own.

He edged further over. 'Don't! You'll fall!'

'Nay,' he answered. 'Moira is holding onto my legs. Trust us, sister. We won't let you fall.'

And they hadn't. Ewan and Moira had pulled her to safety. And, soon, Garrick would bring them to safety too.

A horse whinnied nearby and Garrick brought Montgomerie to a halt and pressed a finger to his lips. Brenna wanted to scream. The cliff was just to her right and now they weren't moving at all. A wave of nausea crushed her. The horizon tilted. She clung tightly to Montgomerie's neck. She drew in a slow breath and the smell of the horse's mane steadied her.

Garrick hadn't moved, his body tense and alert. He stared off to his left, but she couldn't see over the high boulders that blocked her view.

The neigh sounded again, and Garrick eased his blade from its sheath along his waist belt. She ran her fingers along Montgomerie's mane and looked about her for a weapon. It seemed her only real weapon was the horse she sat on. All else was either out of arm's reach or too dangerously close to the edge to risk shifting her weight on Montgomerie for.

Garrick stooped, edged around the lower set of boulders and studied whatever was on the other side of the stretch of rock. Had the attackers found them? Was it another band of soldiers hiding in wait? A band of reivers headed north?

She squeezed her eyes shut for a moment and hoped it was a sweet family travelling to visit relatives in the north, even though she knew it wouldn't be. No family would travel this route. It was too steep and dangerous.

Which was exactly why they shouldn't be trapped here along the precipice.

She bit her lower lip, opened her eyes and prayed. *Provide us an escape. Please.*

After far too long, Garrick's shoulders relaxed and he sheathed his weapon. He nodded to her and tugged Montgomerie along. Soon, they were past the boulders and heading towards the land far away from the cliff's edge. She sighed in relief.

Thank God. She was tempted to jump off the horse and kiss the ground. She hugged Montgomerie's neck instead, and for a moment she could have sworn he pressed his neck back against her as a small sign of reassurance.

She frowned. Lack of food and rest was getting to her.

As they rounded the bend, Brenna started. An old woman was gathering what appeared to be herbs as her horse nibbled on some exposed grass tufts poking out from the snow. What on earth would be growing way up here that one would want to harvest after the first snowfall?

She narrowed her gaze. Was it a trap?

Garrick called a greeting and the petite grey-haired woman stood. She might weigh seven stone in soaking wet wool tartans. Brenna berated herself for her suspicions. She was turning into Garrick and now saw everyone as a threat.

The woman watched them approach. 'Bit far from home, are we?' she asked. Her gaze took in Garrick and then flitted to Brenna. She smiled. 'Wish I could have dressed like such when I was a lass.'

Brenna flushed when she realised the woman was referring to her trews and tunic. She wrapped the plaid tightly around her.

'We're hoping to trade for some supplies and then be on our way. Do you live in these parts?' Garrick asked.

'Depends on what you hope to trade,' she answered, crossing her arms against her chest.

Brenna smothered a smile. She liked this old woman.

He hesitated. 'We have a cross.' He gestured to Ayleen's silver necklace around his throat.

'Nay,' Brenna called out and moved the reins to bring Montgomerie and her closer. 'I have a ring. We'll not trade the necklace.'

Garrick frowned at her.

The old woman eyed it. It was the garnet ring Stephen had given to her as a gift upon her last visit.

Garrick shook his head at her but she ignored him, slid the ring easily off her finger and met the woman's gaze. ''Tis yours if we can have a warm place to sleep for the night, food for us and our horse and something to break our fast in the morn before we depart.'

The woman studied her and then looked to Garrick, as if assessing just how much trouble they might be. 'Aye.' She took the ring, slid it in her dress pocket and nodded. 'We have an agreement. Follow me.'

Garrick came to Brenna and grabbed the reins. 'What are you thinking?' he muttered.

She shrugged. 'The ring can be replaced. I could not allow you to trade away Ayleen's cross. And, like you said, possessions matter little if you are dead.'

He said nothing but took the reins in his hand and began to lead them behind the old woman. She'd tucked away the herbs she had gathered neatly in her saddlebags and clicked her tongue. The mare fell in step beside her as if they'd travelled this very journey a thousand times which, by the grey along the mare's nose, might be true.

The narrow path was well worn and, the deeper they went into the woods, the more Brenna realised that they were on the edges of a small community nestled away from the rest of the world. She spied a granary, drying shed and a well, and then the tops of small stone cottages and makeshift barns. It wasn't a large village, but they seemed to be thriving, despite being nestled so close to the cliffs.

'This is a surprise,' she murmured, and Garrick nodded in agreement.

'Never knew there was a settlement nestled up in here, but I've also never drifted from the trail the few times I have taken it.'

'Who do you think they are? A fractured clan? I see a mixture of plaids.'

'As do I. Let her introduce us to them. I'll not startle them, as we are far outnumbered.' As they entered a more densely settled area, a few men and women paused in their work to watch them walk by.

'Seems a fine plan,' she answered, meeting the uncertain gaze of a woman with a babe snuggled in against her breast. They had enough troubles. The last thing they wished to do was upset the people who might stand between them and survival.

Chapter Nine

'**W**ait here,' the old woman stated, leaving them in the heart of the small village, and approached a man who looked to be the leader of their community. The man's dark eyes watched Garrick as she spoke to him, never taking his gaze from Brenna or him. Garrick held his stare, wondering where he'd seen the man before, as he seemed familiar. He was tall, medium built with thick brown hair that shielded his eyes. The scars along his left cheek were unique, and the haunted look in his eyes as recognisable as Garrick's own in a looking glass. Why could he not place him?

Probably due to lack of food and rest. His mind was not as sharp as it had been in the days before he'd stumbled across Brenna. Before his world had been turned on its blasted end.

The man nodded once, signalling the end of his conversation with the old woman. He walked over to them, stopping at arm's length from Garrick.

'What is your purpose here?' His gaze darted to

Brenna and then back to Garrick. It wasn't lost on Garrick that each of the man's hands rested along his waist belt, at the ready to pull a dagger and defend himself and those in his village if needed. He moved like a soldier, yet Garrick still couldn't place him.

'We are travelling to Oban. We need food, shelter and a night's rest.' Brevity would serve them far more than any details.

'Odd to be travelling along this route.'

'A necessity,' Garrick added. 'We were attacked along the main road to Loch Linnhe. I need to bring her back to family in Oban where she'll be safe.' He chose to leave out any specifics of her clan or family.

'Safe from...?' The man's gaze narrowed on him.

Garrick cursed himself. He'd said too much already, and this man didn't miss the implication that they were in danger. And that the danger might also become their own if Brenna and him were still being followed as they came further into the forest to their village.

He risked the full truth. 'I found her along the road left for dead in an overturned carriage. The attackers have been chasing us since then. I'm trying to protect her and bring her to her family in Oban alive.' He neglected to add that they knew one another. It was important that his attachment to her not become a weakness of his that could be exploited later.

The man's eyes widened, and he shifted in gaze to Brenna. 'Come, then. Flora will get the woman settled. We will talk.'

He turned. Evidently, that was the end of the conversation. Garrick still didn't even know the man's name or if he was friend or foe. Garrick helped Brenna down from Montgomerie and whispered in her ear, 'Do not tell them more than you have to. I'm not sure where we stand.'

She nodded and fell in step with the old woman named Flora as a lad took their horse away to be brushed down and fed. Garrick followed the man to a small cottage made of stone, ever watchful of the other men in the village. None of them followed them inside, but he was being assessed, and he knew it. He steadied his walk, even though he doubted it would disguise his injury.

The man stooped to enter the doorway, as did Garrick. They were of equal size and build. The cottage was warm and well-tended, and he almost sighed aloud when the heat hit his body. The space was sparse but orderly. And everything of import was either near the door or on the small nightstand near the man's bed. He was a soldier, or had been. Garrick was certain of that now.

'You do not remember me, but I remember you.' The man spoke with his back turned to Garrick, exhibiting a show of trust. He wouldn't turn his back on a man he thought might be a threat or deceitful. He added a small log to fuel the winking fire and it glowed back to life. For whatever reason, this man trusted him, even though he couldn't place him. He waited for the man to continue.

'Perth.'

'Perth?' Garrick asked as the man turned to face him.

'Aye. I'm Doran Adair. You saved my life.'

What?

Garrick stilled and set his gaze upon him. After studying the stranger, he shook his head, rubbing his hand over his neck. 'I think you are mistaken. I would remember.'

Doran prodded the embers with a poker to stoke the fire. 'I am not surprised that you don't remember. You were crazed with grief. I believe you saving me was an impulse, a gut response of a seasoned soldier that you thought nothing of. As you might imagine, it meant a great deal more to me.'

He placed the poker aside and leaned against the wall, crossing his arms against his chest. 'Dragged me from the field where the reivers had left me for dead.'

Heat flushed Garrick's body and his heart thudded in his chest.

'Ayleen!' Garrick yelled at the burning abbey. He ran towards the structure and hit a wall of heat and flame he couldn't pass. He jogged alongside it, searching for an opening, any opening, in the fire.

A log popped as the flame consumed it and thrust Garrick back into the present, his heartbeat pounded in his ears.

'I see you remember after all,' Doran observed.

Garrick blinked back the grief threatening to choke him after the intense flash of memory. His breathing was uneven and rapid. He cleared his throat, swallowing the feel of the smoke burning his throat, and shook his head. 'I remember Perth, but not you.' He scrubbed a hand through his hair.

'Aye. Well, perhaps one day you might. Tell me more

about these men following you. I'd like to repay my debt to you.'

Repay me?

If anything, he owed the world for his mistakes, not the other way round.

'I wouldn't trust me either,' Doran added. 'But you are wounded. You and the woman need help if you are to reach Oban alive. It will take you at least two more days by foot and horseback. And if we have more snow it will be longer. And, by the look of you, I do not believe you'll last that long.'

He didn't mince words, which Garrick appreciated. He nodded. 'I know. The past has left me reluctant to trust my instincts.'

Doran laughed. 'I struggled as well after Perth. I ended up here by accident, half-starved, half-dead. Flora's husband took me in, and after he passed I stayed on. I have no family any more, so it seemed the right choice to repay them all for their kindness. They brought my body and soul back from the dead. Since then, I have begun to believe in my instincts again.'

I have no family any more.

The ugly words echoed through him. Nor did he. They had a great deal in common.

'So?' He gestured to the small table and chairs beside them and sat down. 'Will you at least tell me your name? More of what has happened to you and the woman with you? You and I both know it is the only way we can possibly protect you.'

Garrick hesitated, despite feeling ready to collapse.

Please let this not be a mistake. Otherwise, it may

cost Brenna her life, as well as my own. While mine holds little import, hers does. Above all else, I want her to live.

He nodded and walked to the chair. As he sank down and settled in against the smooth wood, relief coiled through him. Doran was right. If they didn't start trusting someone soon, they would both be dead.

Brenna followed Flora at a distance, catching glances of other men, women, and children as she passed. She hugged the tartan around her, self-conscious about wearing his trews and a tunic rather than a gown, as she would and should as a woman in the Highlands. Colour heated her cheeks as many of them took note of this as she passed, their gazes drifting to her legs and then back to her face.

Blast. How much further was it?

Please let Flora have an old gown she could barter for. She still had a nice hairpin that might be worthy of such an exchange. 'Hurry along,' Flora called over her shoulder.

Brenna shuffled and increased her pace, despite her flagging energy. With all of the travel and little food and rest, she was weary. Bone weary. She tripped on a root and almost fell but caught herself before she landed face-first on the ground. Flora paused and waited for her to catch up.

'Best we get some food in ye before ye topple over.' She shook her head and then smiled. 'I've just put on a stew, but I've a loaf and goat cheese for ye until it's ready.'

'And Garrick?' Brenna asked finally, walking side by side with the old woman, who was moving remarkably fast for her age.

'The man yer with?'

'Aye.'

'Doran will bring him round when it is time. 'Til then, ye can eat, bathe and change.'

The implication of a bath and set of fresh, clean clothes made her sigh. 'Thank you. That sounds lovely.' She couldn't keep the wonder from her voice. Had they only been on their own for two days? It felt like a month.

'Name's Flora Hay. Ye are?' she asked as she opened her cottage door.

'Brenna. Brenna Stewart.'

The woman stopped cold in the door frame and faced her. 'Bran's daughter?'

'Aye.'

She shook her head and continued inside. 'Difficult young man.'

'You knew him?' Brenna asked. How could that even be possible?

'Aye. Came through these parts long ago, trying to convince us to be a part of an alliance with his father and clan. Rather sore about it when we declined.'

Brenna chuckled. 'I can imagine he was. He is rather accustomed to getting his way.'

Flora shot Brenna a soft look. 'Not a great lot for a daughter of a laird such as him.'

'Nay,' she answered quietly. 'Not a bit. I find it hard to voice much of anything. 'Tis easier to agree and be agreeable.'

'For the short term, but not the long, lass. Ye are the one living out the rest of yer days, not him. Best ye remember that.'

Brenna bit her lower lip. The truth hurt to hear, and she had no other response than a nod of agreement. She would be living out her days with an Englishman she didn't know, to please Father and her people. Her happiness was a sacrifice she had agreed to. Now, she wasn't even sure why. She should have fought for her happiness, like Moira, or resisted the match, like Ewan. But she had folded to his demands to feel valued.

Now she only felt more worthless.

Flora opened a trunk and pulled out a wool dress, shaking it out. ''Tis wrinkled and a touch big for ye, but it will do far better than being seen in those, even if they are a might bit more comfortable.' She grinned at her. Brenna noticed the gap in her bottom row of teeth and couldn't help but smile back.

'Thank you. I am so grateful.' She pulled a hairpin from her plait. 'Can I repay you for it?' She extended her hand with the hairpin to Flora.

'Nay, child. I'm glad to see it come to some use. My daughter's.' A wistfulness came into her face, and Brenna's stomach tightened. She knew what the face of loss looked like.

'I'm sorry.'

'She is still alive but chooses to live with her husband and new clan up north near Inverness. I'm too old to travel so far, and she doesn't wish to return here. Still misses her father. As do I. Being here makes her sad to remember. I stay because I do not wish to forget.'

Brenna hugged the dress to her chest. What could she say?

'I'll heat some water for ye to bathe with and prepare ye some bread and cheese.'

'Thank you,' Brenna rushed out. The woman was so kind. She reminded her of her mother.

Soon, the basin was filled with hot water and Flora gave her a bar of soap and a small cloth. She stepped behind the hanging sheet for privacy as she bathed. While she couldn't manage to wash her hair, having the chance to wipe off the mud, dirt and stench of the last few days was heavenly.

'Nice looking lad ye have with ye.'

'Aye.' Brenna hesitated, reminding herself not to say too much, as Garrick had warned.

'He give ye that fine ring?'

'Nay,' Brenna answered. 'But he rescued me. I'm grateful of his help to get me to Oban.'

Focus on the truth and only add details if you have to.

'I'd say be warned. The way he looks at ye is familiar. He may be wanting more of a thank ye than ye wish to give.'

Brenna chuckled. 'Flora!'

The old woman gave a hearty laugh. 'I'm not daft, girl. I may be old, but I'm not dead. Not yet anyway.'

'You truly think he fancies me?'

'Aye. And, if I'm not mistaken, ye do too.'

Blast. Do I?

She cringed and squeezed water from the cloth. Aye, she did. More than she wished to admit. She was trying not to care, and to let him go as wilfully as he had her, but her heart pleaded otherwise. Her fingertips tingled at the memory of waking in his arms this morn.

Careful, Brenna. She was meandering into dangerous territory. She shook away the memory that heated her blood.

'As I thought,' Flora said after an overly long pause.

'I didn't say anything,' Brenna sputtered out.

'Ye didn'a have to.'

She cursed and dried herself off. Crafty old woman. Sliding the wool dress over the stays with which Flora had also provided her, Brenna sighed. She was clean, had on fresh clothes and was warm.

While a new pair of shoes might be nice, her slippers would have to do. At least the wool stockings helped. She hadn't realised how numb her toes had been until now. They tingled as she wiggled them and began to get the feeling back.

'Care for yer bread and cheese?'

'Aye,' Brenna answered. Her mouth watered at the sight and smell of it as she emerged from behind the hanging sheet.

She sat at the small table and gulped down a slice of bread before she even realised it. Then she tore another piece in half and ate it with the soft goat cheese. She sighed at the sweet taste of it as it melted in her mouth, thankful for the blessed distraction that filling her belly offered.

Chapter Ten

'We are grateful for your kindness and hospitality,' Garrick said as he and Doran joined Brenna and Flora at the small table in the old woman's warm, cosy cottage. His heart slowed at the comfortable scene of a fire burning in the hearth and the welcoming smells of stew and fresh bread. How long had it been since he'd sat at a table and enjoyed a meal such as this?

He couldn't remember. He sat at the table, met Brenna's gaze and smiled.

'We find that the people who need to find us do,' Flora added, before bringing a spoonful of stew to her lips.

'How so?' Brenna asked, her brow crinkling in curiosity. 'I had no idea this village was here. Nor did Garrick.'

Garrick bit off a chunk of bread and set his gaze upon her. The candlelight flickered along her features, and his chest tightened. He'd almost lost her twice in so many days. Them being here warm and safe with these people was nothing short of a miracle. One that he was thankful for.

'We prefer it that way,' Doran added. 'We call ourselves "the lost village". We are a collection of clans, all displaced or lost by grief. Everyone here has lost a clan, a child, something of significance that drove them away from their home to here. Together, we have found our way back to a life, one we had not imagined for ourselves.'

Garrick swallowed hard. Perhaps his loss, his grief, had led him here. Such a thought seemed ridiculous, but was such a thing possible? Wasn't arriving here a miracle of chance? Or fate? His heart wanted it to be true and wanted to believe that perhaps he had been guided back to Brenna, even after making such efforts to wilfully give her up and set her free, but the warrior in him balked at such a romantic notion. Life didn't work that way.

'A beautiful sentiment,' Brenna murmured. 'I am glad you all found one another and that we found you.'

'Aye,' Garrick added.

While he knew as a soldier that he shouldn't feel so relaxed amongst them, as they were all but strangers, knowing that Doran understood him and his losses, as he'd lost a brother of his own during the battle of the reivers in Perth, set him at ease. Being here with Brenna, knowing that she was warm and cared for, also helped him. They'd been on the run for two days and both of them were bone-weary and starved. He could see it in her drawn features.

'Since the care and aid we were given upon our arrival saved our lives, we like to help others when we can. Such as you.' Flora smiled.

'We will repay you,' Garrick added.

'You have no debt with us,' Doran replied.

Brenna met Garrick's gaze, her eyes narrowed in confusion. He looked away and nodded to Doran. Some debts could never be settled and, while Garrick understood that, he didn't know how to explain it to her without admitting his shame over what had happened to Ayleen, and he was far from ready to do that. Not yet.

If ever.

After enjoying a hearty stew with Flora and Doran, Brenna and Garrick took a walk outside to the barn to check on Montgomerie. Brenna picked up a brush and ran it along the stallion's coat.

'Seems you are being well tended to as well, old boy.' Garrick rubbed the horse's nose, and Montgomerie pushed back his palm in search of more food. 'And yet still greedy for more.'

'Can you blame him? I also ate far more than I should have this eve. My belly is full. They are kind. Perhaps too kind.' Brenna stilled and met Garrick's gaze.

He shifted closer to her. 'I thought the same at first, but it is genuine. I think it is because of how much they have lost.'

Brenna scrunched her brow. 'Aye. Knowing how they all have suffered such losses pains me. It also makes me wonder why they wouldn't feel vulnerable and more prone to protect themselves from strangers like us.' Brenna set the brush down and snuggled deeper into the borrowed cloak that was several sizes too large, making her appear smaller and younger, like when they'd first met.

All he wished to do was hold her. He answered her question instead. 'I think we are both unused to kindness without expectation.'

'You do not believe they will demand something further from us or steal our horse?' she whispered.

'Nay. I don't. My gut tells me so.'

'Are you not nervous to sleep out here alone? Shall I join you?' When she met Garrick's gaze, realising how it sounded, she added with a blush, 'To help you keep watch on Montgomerie, of course.'

Garrick's throat dried. He shoved away the feelings that stirred in the base of his gut that wanted him to say aye. Too much had happened, too much was still standing in the way of getting her to Oban safely. He slammed back his desire for her, and the loneliness that made his longing as sharp as a blade and his limbs prickle.

'Nay,' he finally answered, his throat dry and husky. 'It wouldn't be appropriate. You are engaged.'

And not to me.

'Shall I be worried about staying with Flora?'

He chuckled, relieved by the easy turn in their conversation. 'Are you scared of the old woman?'

She ribbed him in the gut. 'Stop teasing me. We have been through an ordeal. I do not know whom to trust. People are not always as they seem. You know that.'

He cupped her elbow, regretting his words. 'Aye. I

shouldn't jest. You should be wary. I will sleep outside your door to put your mind at ease, if you wish.'

And he would. He would do anything for her. *Always.* And he hated himself for it. She'd chosen another and had already let him go, as he had her. Or at least he thought he had, but seeing her, being with her, was chipping away at his defences.

Letting her go when she was hundreds of miles away had been one thing. Letting go of her now when she was within his grasp was quite another.

'Now who is being addled? You will do no such thing. You will sleep here, where it's warm, and rest. We'll have the opportunity to freeze to death tomorrow after we leave.'

His smile flattened into a line. 'Aye. We will.'

They had at least two more days to Oban, perhaps three if Doran was correct, and the man didn't seem prone to exaggeration. If anything, he might be understating the danger of their journey ahead.

'Then I will see you in the morn.' She gave Montgomerie a last pat and turned to leave.

'I will walk you back.' He rushed out, not wanting to be separated from her yet. He hadn't mustered up the courage to say what needed to be said, and he'd not be able to rest until he did.

His gut churned with each step closer to the cottage door. *Just say it, you coward.*

'Thank you,' he sputtered out.

She turned to him as she walked. The winking light from Flora's cottage cascaded along the fresh coating of snow on the ground a few lengths in front of them as they approached. 'What for? For not asking you to sleep outside in the snow?' A small chuckle resounded in her throat.

He shoved his hands in his trews and cleared his throat, which tightened with every step. Why was it so hard to speak of anything about Ayleen? He clenched his jaw.

'For offering up your ring in place of Ayleen's cross. It was generous of you. I should not have let you do it.'

She halted in front of Flora's cottage. 'The ring is nothing, while I know the cross means a great deal to you. I would never have let you give it up.' Her eyes glistened in the moonlight as she looked up at him. They held all the wonder they used to have when she'd looked at him long ago before he'd left her and disappointed her. And, for a moment, he wanted to seize it and yank them both back to the past, before he'd lost everything. Before they'd lost each other.

When he'd believed in something, and when she had believed in him.

He ran a fingertip around the edge of her ear, the touch of her warm skin sending feathery whispers through his body as he trailed the pad of his finger down the lobe to skim the side of her neck. Every part of his body tightened. *Deuces*. He wanted to kiss her. Needed to kiss her. And the way her lips parted ever so slightly told him he could. Just once more. Then he could tell her why he'd never returned. He could make right all the things that he had done wrong, but he froze.

Just as he had on the day of Ayleen's death. When it counted, he couldn't act. His mouth, his body, were immobilised by emotion and the fear of loss.

A weakness she didn't deserve.

He had to let the past be and let her go. He swallowed all the words his heart wanted to say and let his hand fall away. Emotion flashed in Brenna's eyes before she blinked and stepped back. In a few days, she wouldn't need him. Not in any way. He'd do well to remember such.

'Where are we headed in the morn?' she asked, glancing away.

'We will try a route Doran suggested. He said it is shorter than journeying along the cliffs and less exposed to the weather. It is more travelled, but my hope is that it might be safer for us, as it is wooded and has much cover. If any men are still after you, I doubt they will have any inkling of where we are travelling to.'

'Do you trust him?'

'Aye.'

'I'm surprised. You are not given to trust so easily.'

'Aye. I decided to take a risk and ask for his guidance, since he knows this land.'

'Why? You told me to be as secretive as possible.'

He shrugged. 'Aye. I did not tell you, but I recognised him when Flora brought us to the village. I didn't say anything to you because I could not place him. Once he told me where he knew me from, it came back to me.'

Even though I did not wish to remember.

'Who is he? How do you know him?'

'From my time in Perth along the borderlands. We suffered…equal losses. I dragged him to safety.'

'You saved his life.' Her features softened, and he hated the way she looked at him. As if he was a hero when it could not be further from the truth.

'He saved himself, but I gave him a chance to do so.'

She shook her head. 'You are so unwilling to let anyone thank you, Garrick MacLean. Why is that?' She crossed her arms against her chest and edged closer to him. 'There is no weakness in acknowledging the good you have done.'

'There is if I failed in the most important aspects of my life when it mattered most.'

'Blazes. You are so bull-headed.'

'No more so than you,' he added.

She scoffed. 'I am not.'

'Aye. You are. You need no one. Least of all me.'

She stepped back and her mouth gaped open.

He'd landed a blow. He hadn't intended to, but now that it was said he wasn't sorry. It was the truth. She didn't need him. No one did.

Instead of recoiling and pushing him away as he'd hoped, she came back to him slowly, like a predator stalking its prey—slow, deliberate and with her gaze locked on his. Fire, passion and something else burned bright in her eyes. His heart pounded in his chest.

'One day,' she began. 'You will realise all you have given up. All that you could have had. That we could have had. I *did* need you. I have since the day we met, but it was you that decided you didn't need or want me once you left for Perth. You are changed. You will not allow yourself happiness.'

'Nay,' he finally answered. 'I may have left but it was you that moved on. *You* gave in to your father's demands in some desperate attempt to please him and win his favour, and got yourself engaged to a bloody Englishman who may or may not want you and your family dead in the process. You showed me you didn't need *me* by moving on. Best you not forget that.'

Hurt shone on her pinched features, and she blinked back the emotion filling her eyes.

'I will see you in the morn. The sooner we reach Oban, the sooner I will be away from you. Then, you can wallow all you wish on your own.' She turned and left him.

He followed at a distance to make sure she reached Flora's cottage safely. She exasperated him, but he still…loved her.

His steps faltered at the realisation. Even though she was promised to another. Even though he didn't deserve her. Even though she hated him, all he wanted was to crush her into his arms and kiss the life out of her until she became as soft and willing as she used to be in his arms.

He cleared his throat.

Nay. Think of Ayleen. Your family. Of what happens to those you love.

She was far better off without him.

Perhaps her hate and rage would make it easier in the end. It would make it easier for her to let him go.

He wished it could be the same for him. He would suffer every remaining moment of their journey.

'Come in, child.' Flora slipped her arm through Brenna's and guided her inside.

Garrick nodded to the old woman but said nothing.

When the door closed and the latch fell into place, the feeling of loss echoed deep in his bones.

Brenna shivered. He had been about to kiss her. She'd seen a flash of the old Garrick MacLean. Desire had flared in his eyes, making the moss-green depths glow a bright clover-green just as they'd used to before he'd kiss the very life out of her. But he'd tamped it down and said nothing but a meagre thank-you for offering up her ring rather than Ayleen's cross. They still hadn't discussed why he'd left her and had never bothered to come back or send word. Still she did not have the answers she craved and it had been days.

'Men,' she grumbled under her breath and removed her cloak.

Flora chuckled at her. 'That, my dear, will never change.'

Brenna flushed. *Had she said that out loud?*

'No doubt he'll exasperate ye till the end of yer days, that one.'

'Oh, we're not a couple, Flora.'

Not any more.

Brenna tried to will the colour to subside on her cheeks. Perhaps she could claim the cold had reddened her face.

She chuckled. 'Both of ye.' She shook her head. 'Yer

words say one thing, but yer eyes and bodies say quite another.' She grabbed a large quilt and handed it to Brenna. 'Take it from me. Do not tarry in putting those things back in harmony. Youth doesn'a last for ever.' She snapped her fingers. 'It can be all be gone in a whisper of time.'

Perhaps the old woman could be trusted, and Brenna needed to talk to someone. Garrick MacLean was making her feel addled. 'I am engaged to another,' Brenna offered. 'But there was a time when I thought *we* might be engaged.'

She tsked. 'Ah. Explains it.'

'Explains what?'

'You'll keep looking at the lad that way until ye get 'im out of yer blood.' Flora filled a cup with hot water, added some herbs and handed it to Brenna. 'Drink. It will 'elp yer body heal.'

She frowned at the horrid-smelling tea and the fact that Flora was right. Garrick was still in her blood. Even now, she couldn't stop thinking of him. What was wrong with her? He'd let her go. He'd tried to make the decision about their future for her, just like her father had. Why couldn't she just let him go as easily as he had her?

'How exactly do I do that?' Brenna asked.

'Only ye know.' She sipped from her own cup. 'But, if it were me, I'd march right back to that barn and figure it out. Regrets have a way o' lastin' for ever.'

Brenna drank her tea. She needed to confront him. Ask what she needed to know before she could let him go. But the thought of having to do it exasperated her. He needed to come to her and explain himself, not the other way around. Didn't he? She almost spilled her tea.

'Curses,' she muttered.

'Ah! Careful now. Drink up and I'll read the leaves, child. I've the gift.'

Brenna sputtered at the idea of having her future told but managed to drink the last of the tea. Flora took the cup from her and held it closer to the flames for light. Brenna clutched the folds of her dress in her hands. What would she say? What could she say? Brenna chided herself. They were leaves. She didn't believe in such things. What was she nervous about?

'Ye may not believe, but I'll tell ye what I see anyhow.'

She balked. 'How did you know I didn't…?'

'Shh.' Flora held up a weathered hand.

Brenna sat back in her chair and curled her toes in her slippers. The waiting was getting to her. *Blast.* She pressed her lips together to keep from asking how much longer it would be.

'Hmm. As I thought,' she said, placing down the cup.

'And?'

'Ye won't believe me.'

She shrugged. 'Perhaps not, but what do they say?'

'He is yer love match.'

She covered her face with her hands. 'How did I know you would say something like that? Flora, your leaves are wrong.'

'They never are, but people are.' She gifted Brenna a toothless smile, and she couldn't help but laugh.

'Well, this might be the first time. If there is one certainty, it is that Garrick and I are never getting back together.'

Chapter Eleven

Morning came early. Far too early. Brenna woke to the smell of oats, spices and Flora's humming. Cocooned in warmth, Brenna couldn't move, nor did she want to. Sunlight streamed through the solitary window in the tidy cottage. She yawned and Flora turned to her.

'Wondered when ye would wake. Your lad has already been by.' She stirred the large pot hanging over the fire that burned in the hearth.

What? How had she not heard him? She had always been a light sleeper, but she'd also never been on the run for two days before, and she'd not slept well in the cave or in the abandoned church. She scratched her head and grimaced at the tangled mess her plait had become. Then, she tucked her arm back inside the quilt and snuggled further into its folds. She didn't wish to go anywhere. Not yet.

'He bid me tell ye to ready yerself to leave within the hour.'

A knock sounded at the door.

'Which was an hour past.'

Brenna scrambled up. 'Flora!' she chided and attempted to straighten herself and her hair.

Flora chuckled, winked at her and went to the door. 'A basin of water is behind the sheet. Just ready yerself. I'll tell 'im to wait a spell.'

Brenna rushed through her ablutions and smoothed her hair as she pulled it from its plait. To keep it from unravelling again, she wrapped it into a loose knot at the nape of her neck and rushed back out into the main room. Flora gave her a small loaf of bread and some cheese wrapped in cloth and pressed a kiss to her cheek. 'The lad won't wait much longer,' she whispered. The dual meaning of her words was not lost on Brenna, but she pushed them aside. She had more important things to think upon, such as staying alive.

'Thank you, Flora.' She squeezed the woman in a hug.

'Don't forget yer cloak,' she called as Brenna went for the door. 'And yer boots.'

Brenna stilled at the sight of a pair of worn boots and the cloak she'd worn yesterday.

'I can't take them, Flora. It is too much. I—'

'Nonsense. 'Tis yers. My daughter has no need of them. Not any more. Without them, ye will suffer in the cold. Take them. Please.'

'Thank you. I hope I will be able to repay you one day for your kindness.' Brenna shrugged into the cloak and pressed a final kiss to the woman's soft cheek.

'Listening to yer heart will be payment enough.'

Tears threatened Brenna as Flora closed the door

behind her, but the sight of Garrick's annoyed scowl from atop Montgomerie banished them. Why was he always in such a foul temper?

'Ready?' he asked, studying her.

'Aye,' Brenna answered, avoiding his gaze. She accepted his offered hand, and he pulled her up easily in front of him.

He tugged her back against his chest and the solid warm presence of his body all at once sent a jolt of heat and longing in her, despite how hard she tried to ignore it. She smiled despite herself.

Damn you, Flora, and your tea leaves.

Garrick and Brenna rode out of the lost village as the sun rose against the horizon. The hot pink and orange shades were in gorgeous contrast to the light snowfall and the forest of dark greens and blacks before them. She studied the landscape in hopes of one day finding her way back to this cosy village. Despite it being a brief visit, Brenna would miss Flora. The old woman had had a way of getting under her skin even if she couldn't read tea leaves. Brenna slipped her hand in the pocket of the cloak Flora had given her and felt something cool. She pulled it from her pocket and spied the ring she had offered Flora as a trade for food and shelter.

'Flora,' Brenna muttered and shook her head.

'Aye?' Garrick asked as he turned Montgomerie into the snow-covered forest, settling into a gentle, steady rhythm as they rode. Large evergreens and naked branches of tall oaks canopied them as they went.

'Nothing,' said Brenna. 'Flora slipped the ring we

traded her back into the pocket of the cloak before she gifted it to me.'

The cool wind fluttered Garrick's hair as he turned to her and smiled, his breath coiling up in the air like smoke. 'Good people. I hope to be able to repay them one day for their kindness and generosity.'

'As do I,' Brenna agreed as she slipped the ring back onto her finger. Maybe that was the one thing she and Garrick *could* agree upon.

They rode for hours in silence, stopping every now and then to provide a rest for themselves and Montgomerie. Soon, the sun was high in the blue sky and beginning its descent. It had helped to melt away the snow, and patches of grass and leaves peeked through. She sniffed the air and her stomach rumbled.

Garrick slowed Montgomerie to a halt.

Brenna listened. At first it was nothing but the smell of something cooking. Rabbit, maybe? But then she heard talking, a low rumbling of voices. At least two men were nearby.

Garrick brought a finger to his lips and guided Montgomerie deeper into the forest. The voices stopped and Brenna held her breath. Had the men heard their approach or merely run out of things to say to one another?

Garrick cupped his hand to her ear and whispered, 'Take the reins and ride as fast as you can to the ravine below. If you can't make it there, head to the water. I will find you.'

He slid off and onto the ground without a sound and pressed the reins into her hands. He gave her hands a squeeze and then disappeared into some dense shrubbery before she could utter a word of rebuttal or question him further.

Why did he keep doing this? She shook her head in irritation and ground her teeth. Why didn't he trust her to help him? Why could they never work together as a team? He always wished to rescue her and send her away from the fray. She released a frustrated sigh and then turned down the path as quickly as she could, with the sloshy ground beneath. She spied the ravine below and headed that way.

It didn't take her long to arrive. Garrick appeared minutes later, out of breath.

'Nothing to worry over. Two brothers out hunting.'

She said nothing.

'What?' he asked, resting his hands on his waist belt. 'Why are you scowling at me?'

'Why must you *always* be the lone wolf? You send me off while you tend to whatever threat is about. Although I am not a soldier, I can be of help. Have I not already? We need to help each other to get to Oban. That can't happen if you send me off each time there is a threat. You are wounded.'

'It is not so simple.'

Suddenly, all the times she'd been set aside because she'd been seen as useless because she was a woman, and was also *Brenna*, ignited like fire in her. The dam of emotion she had been holding burst into her chest. 'Aye, it is. If I was a man, I would be asked to assist you. As a woman, I am dismissed despite being capable.'

He blinked back at her, his body still. Frozen, even.

A small slip of movement along his hands resting along his waist belt caught her eye. Then he pulled and threw a dagger in a blink of an eye. It whizzed by her ear, followed by a thud to the ground. She turned to see a dead man behind her.

Shock stifled the scream in her throat. What was happening?

Garrick grabbed Montgomerie's mane, leapt up onto the horse's back behind her and kicked the stallion's sides. The horse sped off, and Garrick covered Brenna with his body as he bent low to shield her. She couldn't breathe. They raced through the fields and up a long embankment. Hooves sounded behind them and Montgomerie took a sharp right turn. An arrow cut into the tree behind her a moment after they changed direction and she gasped.

Were there others? Had it been a trap? She clung to Montgomerie's sides inhaling the deep scent of horse-flesh and earth. Another arrow sunk into a tree near them as they continued. They were close, so close.

Please God, let us live.

'Jump,' Garrick commanded.

She opened her eyes. 'Jump?' she asked, scanning the area. It was a wide-open field. How would she be able to outrun anyone here? And how could he outride them?

'I'm sorry,' he said, and then grabbed her by the waist and let go. She hit the ground hard before rolling to a stop.

Sucking in a breath, she rubbed her thigh before clambering up and running into the forest. With her dark cloak, she'd have a better chance at hiding there until she could work out what was happening.

She scanned the area as she jogged along. *Thank you, Flora.* The woman's gifts of a cloak and walking boots would save her. Ducking behind a large fallen tree, she crouched down and studied the area. Dense woods to the south, open field to the north behind her and less dense woods to the east and west. Surely she should go south towards Oban? She panted for breath and closed her eyes, remembering what Garrick had told her but minutes before.

Head to the water.

She breathed in and out to slow her heart. She'd never be able to hear the water if all she could hear was her heartbeat roaring in her ears. In and out, in and out. Her breathing began to even and then slow. She could do this. Despite being a poor hunter, she had a keen sense of direction and could use what landmarks she had coupled with the sun to find her way out of this mess. But she also had to do all of that while not being killed by those hunting them down with a bow and arrow.

That was another problem altogether.

And then there was finding Garrick. Her heart thundered again. She needed him. Despite what he believed, he also needed her. Without each other, how would they ever get to Oban? Hurried and loud footfalls sounded behind her, as if someone was running towards her, and she held her breath. Crawling on the ground, she peeked out from the side of the log she was hiding behind and saw Garrick coming right towards her with two men running hard and fast behind him.

Where was Montgomerie, or the other men's horses?

Her heart sank. Had they felled Garrick's beloved horse with an arrow, or had he been snared in a trap? Rage bloomed hot and full in her chest. If they had, she would seek out her own revenge, as she'd grown terribly fond of the creature. She searched for a weapon but only found a large, long branch nearby, which was better than nothing. While she couldn't take out both of Garrick's pursuers with it, she could try to trip up one. And if they had hurt Montgomerie that was the least she could do...

Garrick ran past her with one man close behind. Once they passed, she slid out the branch and raised it just as the last man approached. His feet tangled up in it and he hit the ground hard with a groan, sliding on the wet leaves. He caught sight of her and growled. She popped up and ran in the same direction as Garrick. When she spied a tall oak, she grabbed one of the lowest branches and swung herself up. She hopped up to the next branch and then another. While she knew she couldn't outrun the bastard, she could out-climb him. He was far too large and heavy a man to be able to climb.

Don't look down. Don't look down.

That was the only weakness in her plan. She hated heights like she despised bats. She tucked herself as close to the trunk as she could, in case he was the one with the fine bow and arrow skills.

A dagger landed in the bark near her hand and vibrated from the force of the throw, and she scrabbled to keep hold of the tree. It was a near miss, but on the bright side she now had a weapon of her own. She yanked it from the bark and held it. Clinging to the bark, she dared not look below to see where the men were, or even where Garrick was. One glance would send her into a panic, so she stared out at the horizon and the hills far away from where they were now.

Way off in the distance to the south, she could see the outskirts of a small village. Was that Oban? It looked far closer than she thought it would be. If they survived this attack, they could make it there in a day if they pushed hard.

Her heart dropped. That was only if they still had Montgomerie… Her heart squeezed at the thought of losing the beautiful horse, and she wasn't certain they had.

'Ye cann'a hide up there all day, lass,' the man called up, laughing at her.

She scoffed. Little did he know that the idea of coming down this tree was even more terrifying than encountering him. She might very well be up here all night. The tree shook. Hazarding a glance down, she glimpsed the man hoisting himself up to the first branch.

Blast.

He was large and slow in his ascent, but he'd reach her in time. Now what was she to do? And where was Garrick? She'd lost sight of him and his pursuer long ago once they'd disappeared into the distance. Another blade flew up near her leg, missing it but pinning her skirts to the flesh of the tree. *Thistles.* The man had keen aim. She tried to bend over to gather the new blade, but she couldn't do it without looking down, which made her vision swirl. Leaning back against the trunk and gripping it with all her might, she sucked in slow, steady breaths. She could do this.

Useless.

She wasn't useless. She was strong. She was also a Stewart. She would work this out. She closed her eyes, leaned down and felt for the blade and, once she'd found it, she pulled it from the tree, freeing her skirts in the process. Carefully she moved back and balanced herself, taking deep breaths to steady her breathing and think clearly. She needed a plan.

Aye, I can do this.

'Prayers will na save ye now, lassie. I'm coming up.'

What?

She could hear the scraping of boots along bark and grunting as the man began his climb up, branch after branch. *Perfect.* Not only had he reached the second branch, but he was continuing up. She scanned the tree. What could she throw at him to slow his progress? She frowned. The only thing she had other than the daggers, which she might need, was her beloved walking boots. She sighed and stooped to unlace them with one hand while still clinging to the tree with the other.

Possessions won't matter if we're dead.

Garrick had been right yet again, and she muttered to herself.

She waited until the man was in view and hurled the boot at his head.

It hit him soundly on the top of his head, and he

cursed, sliding a length back down the trunk. She congratulated herself on her precision.

'Ye minx. Just wait till I get a hand on ye!'

She cringed as he thrust himself back up and onto the next branch. The man had only two more to go until he would be able to reach up and grab her by the ankle.

She unlaced the other boot, her stockinged feet curling around the branch to steady herself. Patiently she waited until he was in the perfect position to heave her other boot at him. He looked up right as she threw it, so it hit him squarely in the eyes and forehead, eliciting yet another curse.

'Bitch!' He rubbed his forehead. 'Ye will wish ye had never seen me once I get a hold of ye.'

'I fear you may feel the same about me,' Garrick answered. He threw a blade at the man and it hit him square in the back. He hollered and fell from the tree. Brenna turned away to avoid seeing the impact of his fall but winced as she heard the dull thud as the man hit the ground.

She sighed in relief and clung to the tree. 'Sound timing. I had run out of boots,' she called.

'You can come down now,' Garrick answered.

'Aye,' she replied shakily. 'I know that.'

'Well, come on, then. While I think this is all of them from their scouting party, there may well be more on the outskirts, as I'd believed there were only two of them the first time.'

'I don't know if I can come down,' Brenna admitted, daring a glance to see where the next limb was. She swiped her foot in the air.

How had she got up here in the first place? *Thistles*.

'Bren, we've no time for this nonsense. Climb down.'

'I am not being difficult. I'm afraid of heights, as you well know.'

He paused. 'Then how did you even get up there?'

Exasperated, she shouted back, 'I don't know. I just did. I looked up and climbed. A man was trying to kill me, if you will remember. I suppose I was more frightened of him than the height.'

Garrick uttered a curse and then the tree shifted. She stole a glance to see him climbing up one branch after another. She hated being rescued. She had to at least attempt to go down one limb just to salvage some of her withering dignity.

You can do this. You can do this.

She leaned back, let her hands slide carefully down the bark and let her back foot fall until it touched one of the branches below. She slid down and rested there. Her heart hammered in her chest, her body vibrating from the effort of descending such a short distance.

'See,' Garrick encouraged. 'You can climb down. Try another, Bren. I believe in you.'

His words stole her breath.

Did he believe in her? Why? No one else did.

'I'm only a branch below now. Step down onto the last branch and we can climb down the rest together.'

We can climb down the rest together.

Tears threatened and she bit her lip. Why did his words hit her so squarely in the chest, making it so difficult to breathe?

He wasn't talking about anything other than getting down from this tree. She was promised to another. He didn't love her. She didn't love him. Not any more.

Did they?

Yet, she felt sick to her stomach, knowing they never would be much of anything together any longer, and she didn't even know why. That was a lie. She did know why. He'd never told her why he'd disappeared and never returned. Why he'd never fought for her. Why he'd let her go without a word. He had been the centre of her belief in the world and in herself, and when he'd gone and disappeared without a trace what little hope and belief she'd had in herself had blown away in the wind.

And it made her furious.

She battled back her tears and clenched her jaw. She would get down from this blasted tree and get answers. Demand them. She deserved to know why. She deserved to be able to close that chapter of her life neatly and move on.

And knowing the truth would make her feel better.

Until then, she'd focus on her anger to get down.

She leaned back, let her leg fall out and swing until it landed on another limb below. Lowering herself down again, pride filled her chest. She had done it.

'Good.' Garrick smiled and hoisted himself onto the branch with her. He was so close, his chest pressed to her back.

She'd done it all right. *Perfect.* Crushed limb to limb against the man she hated one minute and desired the next.

'Face me,' he murmured, resting his palms on her

shoulders, the heat of him easing into her limbs like a sip of whiskey on a cold winter night. She turned in his arms, his hands sliding along her arms to steady her, leaving a trail of heat and fire. He loosened his waist belt and looped it around her before buckling it again.

'Hold on,' he whispered, synching the belt around their waists, his eyes flickering with desire. A shock went through her body at the jolt of movement that thrust them closer to each other. He guided her arms up and around his neck until his lips were flush with her forehead.

Did he just kiss her?

She had to have imagined it.

One branch and then another, and she clung to him, squeezing her eyes shut.

The ground. All she wanted was to be back on the ground.

And to never leave his arms again.

She stilled at her own thoughts. What was wrong with her? She needed to get her feet well on the ground. Being this high in the air was making her addled. The man was going to give her answers for what he'd done to her and why.

Now.

Otherwise, she would shift back and forth for ever between what had been and what could be, and that was no way to live a life or a future, especially after almost perishing up a blasted tree.

Chapter Twelve

'Better?' Garrick asked as he jumped from the last branch to the ground and settled her there alongside him. He loosened his belt from her waist, his hands lingering along her sides. His chest tightened as she stepped away from him, creating a void. His body thrummed at the loss of her. She'd always had this effect on him. Since the day they'd met, he'd felt in harmony with her on every level, and when they'd been separated he'd felt incomplete.

And everything in his life lacked colour.

How in the world could he give her over to another man, knowing how incomplete he would feel for the rest of his days?

He sighed and brushed off his hands on his trews. Because it was what was best for her. He couldn't protect her, and the idea of trying to and failing once more, of losing her as he'd lost his family, gutted him more than his desire for happiness. She mattered to him more than he mattered to himself.

Letting her go was the right thing to do. The just thing to do. She deserved a whole man to be her husband, not him. He was shattered into a thousand pieces.

'Why on earth did you toss me from Montgomerie? And where is he? Did they…?' Her face paled.

'He should be fine. I hid him by the water.'

'And you shoved me off and left me because…?'

'To keep you safe.'

'You left me alone and forced me to climb up a tree to escape when I hate heights to keep me safe?' Anger darkened her blue eyes into something close to a bluebird's wings.

He paused. He'd missed something. 'Why are you angry at me for protecting you?'

'Abandoning me, again, does not keep me safe.' She shook her head and gathered her boots, muttering to herself as she went.

He gritted his teeth. 'You are safe and alive, so I must disagree.'

'But for how much longer? If we don't start working together and staying together, we may not make it to Oban. As a soldier, you should know that.' She yanked on a boot and tied the laces.

He scoffed and rested his hands on his waist belt. 'Do you want me to keep you by my side to fight?'

'We could at least help one another. You just assume I will be of no use and cast me aside.'

'Can you throw a blade? Fight off a man twice your size?' He shook his head. 'You aren't being reasonable. Gather your other boot and let's be off.'

Unbelievable. Had *he* just called *her* unreasonable?

She couldn't let it go. He was finally talking with her, and she'd ask what she'd wanted to ask since the day he'd rescued her and been thrust back into her life. And this time he would answer it.

'Is that why you left me, abandoned me, a year ago? I was of no use to you?'

He stilled. The blood drained from his face.

'I will not leave here until you answer me. I deserve that at least.'

He rubbed the back of his neck and released a sigh. 'Because I had to.'

She shook her head, but then met his gaze, fire burning in her eyes. 'Nay. That is no answer. You are a laird. You do not have to do anything at all. The world bends to you like reeds in the wind. You could have stayed. You could have returned. You chose not to. Admit it.'

His blood hammered through his veins. Anger flashed through him. 'You know nothing of what the world has or has not given me. The world has never bent to me, Brenna, as it has to you. *I* have lost everything, not you. We're leaving.' He stalked off and down the hill in search of where he'd left Montgomerie before he lost his temper.

'By all that is holy, do not walk away from me, Garrick MacLean. You will finally explain to me why you left.' She ran to catch up with him. 'I will know the truth.'

'None of it matters. It is the past.' He watched the distance, scanning for trouble as he went, doing his best to ignore her protests and demands. 'Keeping you alive is what matters now.'

'And the only way we can stay alive is if we work together, and we cannot do that with this wedge between us. You must explain yourself. Otherwise, how can we trust one another?'

Garrick hesitated to answer. Was that the sound of horses galloping off in the distance? He cursed and hunched over to shield her as he dragged her along to a large set of boulders to their left.

'There are more,' he muttered.

'I thought Doran said this was the safer route.'

'It is.' Garrick stared out in the direction they had just come from.

He turned and eased his head up and over the boulder. *Curses.* He recognised the plaid from earlier in their journey. While the MacLeans had always been in good standing with the Camerons, the Stewarts had a rather precarious relationship with the dominant clan that butted up against their borders to their north. 'Has your father mended his issues with the Camerons?'

'Nay. He has ongoing skirmishes with quite a few clans. You know this.'

'Have the Camerons begun working with the King?'

'Nay,' she scoffed. 'They wield too much power. They have no need to. Not *that* much has changed since your departure.'

'But they are too far south. Why would they be here in these woods?'

She shrugged. 'The Camerons are everywhere. Perhaps they have eased further south. This land was abandoned by the MacDougalls after their laird passed and had a less than spectacular harvest last season. They moved in closer to the sea.'

'Why didn't you tell me?'

'You didn't ask,' she snapped. 'You were too busy throwing me off horses and keeping me safe.'

Damn. Now they had to deal with the Camerons. The soldiers on their horses approached. They'd been seen. Otherwise, they wouldn't have headed this way.

He pulled a blade from his boot and handed it to Brenna. 'Stick it up your sleeve. Be ready to throw it if need be. Perhaps you'll have fine aim twice.'

'Show yourself. You hunt on Cameron grounds.'

Garrick stood with his hands out. 'Nay. We are travelling through. We are not hunting, and upon last check these are not Cameron grounds.'

'The men with you were hunting. You cannot deny it.'

Garrick took note of the fact the man did not contest the challenge to these being Cameron grounds. 'Aye. They were hunting and tried to kill us in the process. We killed them to escape. We are travelling to Oban. We have no quarrel with you.'

'And you are?'

'Garrick MacLean, Laird of Westmoreland.'

The man stilled and studied him, narrowing his brow. 'You are dead.'

The soldier next to him pulled back his bow and arrow, ready to set it free straight into Garrick's chest at the leader's command.

'Nay. Just presumed to be. I returned to find my home and family dead. I am trying to bring this lass safely to Oban to be with her family. She was left for dead by a band of raiders along the road.'

'And the girl?' The man approached, gesturing to the boulder.

Garrick studied the man, hesitating to reveal Brenna to them. He did not know if he could be trusted. He didn't even know who he was.

'And you are?' Garrick countered.

'Rolf Cameron, son of Laird Cameron.'

Garrick smiled in relief. 'We have met, but when you were but a boy. I remember you had a fine hound. I came and hunted one summer with you and your brother, Royce, to thin the herd of deer.'

The young man studied him and recognition dawned on his face. 'Aye. That was a while ago. Ten years? But I do remember. Father scolded me for sneaking out to follow the hunt. Almost got shot by an arrow.' He nodded and the soldier next to him put down his bow and arrow and slung the pouch of quivers and bow behind his shoulder.

Garrick chuckled, relieved by the reduced threat. 'I remember. You were about the same size as the deer at the time.'

Rolf nodded. 'Aye. I was.'

'We would be grateful for safe passage through your lands. We are trying to reach the McKennas of Westmoreland.'

'Aye. We have an agreement with Laird McKenna. We will assist you.' He whistled and twenty soldiers emerged from the trees as if they had materialised out of the bark.

Garrick stilled. *Saints be.* He hadn't seen any of them. The Camerons were skilled warriors and always had been. Luck smiled down upon them. If Rory hadn't had such an agreement with them, Garrick and Brenna might have already been felled by an arrow.

'So, who is this lady you travel with?'

'Bran Stewart's youngest daughter, Brenna. You can come out now,' he called.

Slowly, she emerged from behind the boulder, her gaze fixed upon Rolf. 'We are acquainted,' she answered coolly.

'Aye.' Rolf frowned. 'We are. How is your brother?'

'Ewan is well. And your shoulder?'

Rolf shifted on his feet and rested his hands along his weapons belt. 'Healed. Although we are still awaiting repayment for the stallion lost by his carelessness.'

Deuces. Garrick commanded himself not to roll his eyes. What had Bran and Ewan done now to incite the wrath of one of the most dominant clans in the Highlands?

'I am certain the Laird of Glenhaven and his son will take care of that outstanding debt upon our safe return. Is that not right, Miss Stewart?' Garrick met her gaze, willing her to be agreeable so they might live to see Oban.

She hesitated but then nodded. 'An oversight on their behalf. My recent engagement has been a distraction.'

'Congratulations,' Rolf added. 'I had not heard.'

'Aye. It has been swift in its terms.' Garrick was thankful she did not add the bit about being engaged to an Englishman.

'Then I wish you the best upon your union.' He nodded to Garrick.

'Nay,' Brenna added. 'Tis not with Laird MacLean.'

Garrick clenched his jaw, willing her to say no more.

''Tis an Englishman.'

Rolf shook his head and muttered to himself as he turned. 'Bloody hell. Let us go before I change my mind.'

Garrick fell in step with him and waved Brenna on to join them. 'Aye. A fine idea. We are grateful for your assistance. Our journey has been challenging. I will need to stop along the stream to gather my mount.'

Rolf whistled and another man emerged from the forest, holding Montgomerie's reins. 'We have already found him. It alerted us to the situation at hand, as we have a daily sweep through this pass. It is often travelled by hunters and thieves, so we keep close watch.' His gaze slid to Brenna and then back to Garrick.

Garrick shook his head. *Of course they would.* They had the men and the means to do so. One of the few clans of the area that did. 'Aye. Thank you.'

Despite being in the hands of the Camerons, a thread of relief spooled through Garrick. They were aligned with the McKennas and would protect them because of it. No doubt it was the only reason Rolf and his men hadn't seized them already for trespass. Garrick grimaced. He was bone-weary and his wounds ached from the strain of the battle with the men they'd encountered along the way. If Brenna could keep from inciting the Camerons, they had a chance of finally reaching Oban, where Garrick could fulfil his duty of returning her safely to the fiancé waiting for her and be on his way to attempt to salvage his clan and have his revenge.

'And if we could send word to the Laird of Blackmore, so he will know of our arrival…?'

'Aye. That shall be no difficulty.'

'And Father?' Brenna asked.

Rolf's steps hitched for a beat but then he continued. 'Aye, my lady. If that is your wish.'

Garrick sent her a glare. She lifted her eyebrows at him in challenge.

He counted to ten in his head, reminding himself to be patient. He was hungry, tired and aching, and not at his best. Losing his temper would not do anyone a whit of good. Not when they were so close to reaching Blackmore safely and putting this behind them. Then, Brenna could be back on track to living the life and future she wanted, and he could begin the task of attempting to put what was left of his back together.

Even though he had no idea how to begin. How did one begin a life again without a family, clan or home to their name? His gut turned. One couldn't when there was nothing left to piece back together. Perhaps he would just return to the field as a soldier. He was good at it and the losses didn't plague him as they used to. He could even assemble a few wayward men to help eradicate the bands of reivers running rogue through the borderlands unchecked. Doran might even join him in that endeavour. He'd had losses of his own, ghosts that still haunted him as well. One of the many reasons they'd understood one another.

He thought of asking Rolf if he knew of the lost village, but if the man didn't Garrick would be exposing his new friends to being absorbed by one of the most powerful clans in the Highlands, and he couldn't risk such. He'd keep their existence to himself. He could only hope Brenna knew to do the same.

'We have a small lodging off to the south a half-day from here,' Rolf continued.

As Garrick studied the area, he realised it was familiar. He'd been here before many, many years ago as a young boy. 'Is this not MacDougall land?'

Rolf didn't answer for a moment, as if choosing his words carefully. He nodded towards two men far ahead of them. 'Aye,' he replied, his voice low. 'Their clan was overrun and the laird stripped of his title. Its members scattered and left to fend for themselves.' He paused, his jaw tightening. 'Much like yours.'

Garrick's steps faltered and he cleared his throat.

Much like yours.

So the MacLeans were not the only ones to be made an example of. He clenched his hands into fists at his sides.

'Laird McKenna and my father decided to band together and protect this area between us as best we could. There are still hunters and thieves about, but we will soon restore it to what it once was with the proper men and coin. And time, of course.'

'Aye,' Garrick answered. His throat was tight with anger and emotion. The King had no right to obliterate the clans bit by bit. One day the bastard would answer for what he'd done. Garrick only hoped it would be within his lifetime.

Rolf met his gaze. 'Father says we will have our day. And we will. But we are far from strong enough yet.'

'The day shall never be soon enough.'

'Use it to fuel you, brother,' he whispered. 'Otherwise, it will eat you alive.' The pain in his dark gaze told Garrick that he understood the words he said, as he had lived him. 'I will check on the men. Ride if you wish.' He whistled and one of the Cameron soldiers brought over Montgomerie while Rolf jogged away to catch up with the men at the front line.

Garrick took the reins and rubbed Montgomerie's nose. 'Aye, boy. Almost there.' He mounted and extended his hand to Brenna.

She hesitated.

'Whatever qualm you have with me we shall settle this eve. Until then, we ride.'

'And if I don't?'

'In case you missed the ire in Rolf's eyes, you are not revered here. I am the only ally you have until we reach Oban. Just be glad your brother-in-law is so well liked that they didn't cleave us with a dozen arrows.'

'You make a point.' She accepted his hand, and Garrick pulled her up to settle in front of him.

The rest of the afternoon was uneventful. Merely a quiet ride through what Garrick could now see was clearly a clan that had been burned out of its village, its crops torched along the way. Skeletons of cottages dusted in snow, half-fallen rock walls and the small graveyard with its markers off in the distance.

Brenna shivered against him.

'Are you cold?' Garrick asked, pulling her closer to him on instinct.

'Nay,' she whispered. 'It is eerie to travel through. So many empty remnants of the lives that were once here.'

'Aye.' He hesitated. 'Is this what became of villages below Westmoreland? Of my clan?'

Her silence was his answer. He sucked in a breath, and she placed her hand briefly upon his and squeezed it before letting go.

The gesture was almost his undoing, and he cleared his throat to keep the emotion at bay. His people had suffered this. On his watch. He faced the ruins. He would not look away at the carnage. He studied everything. The broken cookery, the scorched roof of the small house, even the burnt remnants of a plough, its iron ploughshare and beam tilted and wedged in the ground.

This would keep him focused on his mission: return Brenna and restore his clan. He didn't want to lead it any more, as he had lost such a privilege by abandoning it before, but by all that was holy he would restore his people. He would find them a home and future to live for. Somehow, he would do it, and these images would push him on until he was nothing.

The King would not win.

'Whatever you are thinking, Garrick MacLean, don't.'

Brenna's words yanked him back from his thoughts. 'You do not know me so well,' he muttered. 'To claim to know my thoughts.'

'Actually, I do, and I am reminding you that you cannot undo the past. You cannot bring any of them back.'

Her words landed like an anvil to his chest, squeezing out the temporary hope his anger brought him.

'Nay, I cannot, but I can bring the men who did this to their knees.'

Chapter Thirteen

Of course, Garrick would focus on retribution. Brenna stared out as the muted orange rays of the sun began to set over the dark, reflective mirrors of the sea that had finally come into better view. She hugged her cloak to her body. Was that not what all men did? Died for past deeds and sacrificed themselves in the name of the dead, only to unwittingly abandon the living? She was so tired of it. Bone-weary of never looking forward. All she wanted was to seize her chance, her moment of freedom and happiness, but she seemed destined to have it slip from her grasp.

Again.

First, she'd believed Garrick would be her hope for the future. That they could secure it together and build a family and something of substance on their own. When that had faded away into nothing when he'd disappeared, and after she had grieved, she'd seized upon the idea of marrying Stephen Winters, as it would bring some security to her clan. She was beginning to understand why Moira had not wished to remarry at all after her first husband's death and had wanted to live unburdened in a garden surrounded by her wee plants. For years all she had wanted was to be pretty and sought over enough to have suitors to choose from and make Father proud of her by achieving a suitable match that would enhance the clan's power in the Highlands.

She'd been such a fool.

No wonder she had been viewed as useless. A suitable match was the goal of a girl in braids, not the goal of a woman who desired independence and worth.

Maybe having Garrick leave her had been a saving grace. She'd learned to sew—not well, mind you—but she could. She had learned some healing techniques and the importance of herbs. All to prove to herself and others that she was more than pretty Brenna in lovely frocks without a care in the world or a meaningful opinion in her head. That she had worth, like her siblings.

But the moment Garrick had returned she'd realised that those goals had also been a ruse to distract herself from the truth at hand. She still had no footing, no understanding of what she truly wished to be or what mark she wanted to make in this world. She was not settled in the future, working towards her goals like her sister and brother. She was tethered to nothing and could blow away, disappearing into nothing if the right wind blew her about, and it threatened to drive her mad.

They made a final turn to what appeared to be an old barn. Its high ceilings and wide shape suggested it was little more than a structure built to break the wind and protect one from the elements. As the wind ruffled the edges of her cloak against her face, casting prickles of cool snowflakes on her cheek, she was grateful to know she would not be forced to sleep out in the cold. And even more excited by the prospect of being at Blackmore tomorrow eve. She could sleep in a warm bed, have a bath, see her sister again and not be forced to be in constant contact with Garrick, the man she still…

'Did you hear me?' Garrick asked, resting his hand on her own, sending a trill of attraction through her.

She shook her head, angry at herself for still mooning over a man who did not love her. Why could her body and heart not forget him when he had so easily forgotten her?

'You can go inside. I'll tend to the horses.' He turned to Montgomerie and Rolf came over, offering to assist her down. She accepted his hand reluctantly, but she was grateful for his strength, as she felt weak in the knees as her boots hit the snow.

'Go on in. They will have built the fire by now.'

'Aye. Thank you,' she answered gratefully. And she was. Her teeth chattered in her skull. Her belly grumbled with hunger. Her limbs ached from journeying over several days.

When she entered the structure, the warmth and size of it stunned her. There was a large set of stalls on one side for animals, an open area in the middle with a hearth and tables with benches and living quarters off to the right. She'd never seen such a place before and she stood taking it all in.

'Your brother-in-law helped us build it. A way station of sorts, for travellers as well as us when we make our sweeps of the hillside. He is generous as well as ingenious.' Rolf stood beside her.

'I would agree. He is a good man.'

'So is Garrick. Best not take advantage.'

She balked. 'What are you talking about?'

'I believe we understand each other perfectly, despite your words.' His scowl deepened as he studied her face.

Before she could challenge him further, Garrick came in and approached them. 'Quite a place you have here, Rolf. We are grateful for your generosity.'

'Thank Rory. It was his idea and coin.'

'I will, but you gave us safe passage. It will not be forgotten.' He clapped him on the shoulder.

Rolf smiled. 'Let us get you all the way to Blackmore before you give us any further praise. There are two makeshift beds on the far end. She should take the higher one.'

'Thank you.' He nodded and led Brenna to the wooden slats that acted as beds and the wool blankets covering them. 'We are lucky to have run into them and made our way to this shelter. It would have been a cold night otherwise.'

'Aye.' She avoided his gaze and shifted away from him. 'I will tend to my needs and return.' She couldn't be near him a moment longer or she'd scream.

'I'll come with you,' he offered.

Garrick followed Brenna outside. After getting her this far, he'd not abandon her now and leave her exposed. While he didn't believe those who had originally been after her were continuing their hunt, he didn't know what else or who else lurked outside in this storm.

As he followed her, she stopped and faced him, crossing her arms against her chest. 'Tell me the truth behind why you abandoned me or leave me be.'

He blinked back at her. Just when he thought he'd avoided the previous conversation, Brenna revived it once more. 'I am looking out for you. I know you are tired. We all are. Stop being so unreasonable.'

Her eyes widened and he knew he had made a misstep. 'Unreasonable? Am I really?'

'Aye,' he answered, closing the distance between them. 'What has you so riled?'

'You. You will never understand me.' She moved deeper into the evergreens as a light snow began once more, its flakes glittering along her dark cloak.

Garrick rushed after her. What was wrong with her? She couldn't run into the forest alone. Not with who knew what about. Grasping her by the arm, he forced her to stop and look at him. 'Will you…?' The rest of the sentence died on his lips. The tears he saw falling unbidden down her cheeks gutted him, and he stood transfixed.

'I hate you, Garrick MacLean. I curse the day I met y-you.' She hiccupped on the last word.

And the day I met you was the best day of my life.

He shook his head, his heart slamming in his chest. Alarm bolted him to the ground. Something was very wrong. Brenna didn't cry. The only time he'd seen her cry before was…the day he'd left.

'I am not trying to be obtuse. I am trying to return you to the life you want. The one you chose.' He gripped her by the arms.

'Why did you abandon me? Just tell me. Stop torturing me by not answering when I ask.'

'You know why,' he answered.

'Nay. I don't.'

'I left for Ayleen.'

'I know why you left, but why did you not return? Send word? Or let me go? Why keep me bound to the unknown?'

'It does not matter now. That is the past.' He edged closer.

And it didn't matter, not to him. The outcome had been the same. He'd lost her. Did they need to name how?

'It matters to me, yet you will not tell me. You torture me with your silence and stoicism, and I hate you for it.'

He let her arms go. Tortured her?

'How do I make you understand?' she pleaded.

'Just try,' Garrick rasped out. His throat tightened. If they were to both survive losing one another, they needed to move through the past and let each other go, even if it obliterated him to bits.

'For the longest time, I never felt I was enough, but with you...*you* made me realise *I* was enough. I didn't have to prove anything else to anyone. I didn't have to try to please Father, or be smart like Moira, or follow duty to the clan like Ewan. I was enough as me... Brenna.' She pressed a palm to her chest, tears streaming down her cheeks.

'But you left me and never came back, and all I could conclude was that I wasn't enough. And I hated you for it. I hated you for letting me believe that I was enough for just one moment. Because, when I realised I wasn't, I couldn't breathe. I couldn't be. I was lost.'

Her body shook. 'So that, Garrick MacLean, is why I hate you and why, now that you have come back, I hate you even more.'

By God, she was beautiful. Had she ever been more beautiful to him than now, covered in mud and dirt, her cheeks coloured with emotion? Emotion for him. All he wanted to do was crush her into an embrace, but he didn't dare move lest he startle her like a doe in the brush.

He had broken her. He'd never felt as small as he did now, knowing he had brought her to this. He also knew it was but another example of why he needed to let her go. He was clumsy with those he cared for, especially fragile bits of beauty such as her. How could he make her understand it was him, not her?

'I left you and I had planned to come back. I did. I just needed to save Ayleen, because I couldn't save my brother Lon from the fever that stole him from us too soon. You know that. You remember.' He released a shuddering breath before continuing.

'But, when I couldn't save her, I was lost. I realised I wasn't enough for you to keep you safe. Because what brother can't protect his baby sister? What brother encourages her to follow her heart and to enter the church, where she is then murdered by reivers? Who does that?'

She stared at him.

'Do you need a man like that, Brenna?' he challenged, edging closer to her. 'A man like me. Broken. A shell of a man who might have been good enough for you long ago but is no longer. Because I hate myself for not saving Ayleen. And then to return and learn that I stayed away from what was left of my family to protect them, only to find them dead anyway? That maybe I could have stopped it, but I made yet another bad decision and failed them by not being here?

'How could I ever be the man worthy of protecting you, the woman I love most in this world? How can I make you understand that? So, it wasn't me abandoning you, Brenna. I was trying to give you a better chance at happiness with someone else who was worthy and able to protect you. Not someone broken and unable like me.'

Brenna shook her head slowly and her chin trembled.

'But that was not your decision to make! You cannot simply decide for me.' She grabbed a fistful of his tunic in her hand, tugging him to her.

His body ached with the need, want and anguish that only her touch and kiss could ease, but he held himself at bay, holding his arms by his side despite how he longed to pull her into a tight embrace.

'Look at me,' she demanded.

He didn't dare.

'Garrick,' she sobbed. Her body hitched and the emotion in the sound of his name flooded his chest.

He met her gaze, unable to obey his body's command, her pale blue eyes wide and bright with emotion against her cheeks flushed pink with chill. His resolve burst and he pulled her against him, crushing her mouth with his own. He kissed her over and over again, ignoring the voice that warned him to stop. The one that said he broke everything of beauty.

She pulled him closer and he stumbled back, landing hard against the bark of a tree. Now that he had a taste of her, he could not stop. His body flared with the memories of holding her, kissing her, as they had on so many nights like this in the past.

When she had been his. She could still be his. She tugged his shirt out of his trews and slid her hands along his bare chest, sending a jolt of desire screaming through his body, and he groaned. Pulling her closer, he kissed her again and again, making him believe they could be one again. She tugged on his trews. The action thrust him back to the present, and his desire to the past.

'Bren,' he pleaded, her nickname fallen unbidden from his lips as he clutched her by the wrist, pulling her hand away. 'We must cease. You are engaged to another and I am…'

Me. Not good enough.

He didn't finish but stepped back, creating some distance between them. It didn't matter that his body quaked from the loss of her touch, and his breath came out in uneven, shattering spasms. All he really wanted to do was make love to her, but he froze and let her slip away. Just as he always had.

He cleared his throat and ran a hand down his bunched tunic. 'I shouldn't have kissed you. I'm sorry.'

'Nay. You shouldn't have.' Her eyes flashed in challenge. 'Not if you couldn't finish what you started.'

Deuces. His blood boiled. Aye, he could finish it, but he'd not fall into her bait. He rolled his shoulders and released a breath. They needed to survive, and they could only do that by trusting one another more than they were now, and by him keeping his distance.

'I need to get you back to safety in Oban with your sister and Rory. Then, we can reach out to this fiancé of yours, as well as your father, to determine what is going on and why those men were after you. Your safety is all that matters. You have a life without me already planned, remember? My purpose right now is to get you safely back to that life and I need us to work together to do that.'

And I need to keep my hands off you to do that.

Colour flushed her neck. He'd made his point.

'I had to make my own life, as you well remember!' she snipped back.

'Aye,' he answered, his gaze settling on her. 'And all I want to do is get you to that life in one piece. That will give me an inkling of purpose. Let me do that and I'll be out of your life. For good.'

'Very well,' she whispered. Her features softened, and his heart squeezed from the truth that maybe, just maybe, she had decided to let him go.

That she might give him exactly what he asked for.

Chapter Fourteen

'Time to leave,' Garrick said, shaking her arm.

She blinked her eyes open to see the high-beamed ceiling overhead and the flickering of the dim candlelight in the old barn. She turned and saw the fire was being smothered in the hearth and soldiers were busily packing up their bed rolls and saddlebags. She groaned. Her head pounded and her eyes were scratchy and dry, no doubt swollen from her emotional undoing of the night before. Garrick stared at her, awaiting her response.

'Aye,' she answered. He nodded and carried on with packing. Curse Garrick and his stoic 'nothing happened the night before' face, void of feeling this morning.

Blast. Why should she expect anything else? Garrick was steady, even and dependable. He was a soldier. He could compartmentalise his emotion and move on to the next task, the next battle, the next town without a hitch in his step. Although before he'd utilised it when he'd needed it during difficult decisions. Now, it seemed the very fabric of who he had become. He was void of extremes as well as emotion. He'd become a soldier first and a man second, not the other way around, as it had been.

She climbed down the small ladder that joined the higher makeshift bed to the floor. She smoothed her skirts and yawned. Well, at least she finally knew why he'd abandoned her, even though it didn't make a whit of sense to her. She'd never doubted his ability to protect her or whether he was a good man, but he had enough doubt for the both of them. He couldn't let go of his grief and shame, and she couldn't be with a man who hadn't chosen her and might abandon her once more. She could let him go for good now and move on towards her future to become Mrs Winters.

She sighed and stretched her back. It ached from the makeshift bed she'd slept on. While it was better than the ground, it was no feathered or hay mattress. Tonight would be bliss. Her body sung at the thought of being safe and snug at Blackmore with her sister.

A flutter of nerves bubbled up in her, and she nibbled her lower lip. It had been far too long since she'd seen Moira, and she didn't know of her upcoming nuptial with Stephen. Chances were she would congratulate Garrick and her on being the happy couple when she saw them, unless the letter or Rolf Cameron had bothered to explain such. And, knowing how little Rolf thought of her, the man most likely hadn't. He might even enjoy watching the moment Moira learned of the truth.

Brenna cringed at the awkward moment that such

a revelation would bring. The shock would be evident on her sister's face. Brenna did not look forward to that explanation. Perhaps she could just let Garrick's face do the talking. She frowned, gathered her hair back in a loose plait and shoved her boots on her feet. In half a day their journey would be over, and Garrick would have fulfilled his duty and be out of her life for good. She should be relieved, but all she felt was a dull ache in her chest at what could have been if he'd just had the nerve to fight for her, for them.

For us.

But it wasn't that simple, was it?

She collected her cloak, left the building, completed her ablutions and joined Montgomerie and Garrick.

'Did you break your fast?'

'Nay. I'm not hungry.'

''Tis a long ride,' he answered, tightening the saddle-bags. He handed her a strip of dried meat. She took it, her fingertips tingling from the brief contact with his.

How would she make it several more hours riding alongside him after all she knew from yesterday? She still had so many questions as to why he'd been so quick to decide her future for her, like her father, by letting her go without a word between them. And then his kisses. They'd told a quite different story. Her body warmed at the memory of his hands and lips searing a trail of want along her body. He hadn't kissed like a man who wanted to let her go.

He'd kissed her like a man who loved her.

It would be a long last stretch to Blackmore. He pulled her up in front of him and she settled back, knowing full well that this would be their last ride together—perhaps even their last few hours, if he had his way and left immediately in search of what was left of his clan and those who had killed his mother and brother.

The morning air was crisp and cool, the latest snow having ceased during the early morning hours, leaving a pristine, fresh covering before them. A band of Cameron soldiers rode in a loose V in front of them, the only noises the sound of hooves swishing in the new snow on the ground and the slight jangle of metal on metal from saddlebags and weaponry as they travelled. Despite being pressed against Garrick's body as they rode, Brenna felt more distant from him than ever. There had been a time when she would have thought it impossible and their separation against nature itself.

What a lovesick fool she had been.

Now here she was on a last journey with him when their time together had scarce begun. Fate had other plans, it seemed, and she didn't like the detour at all. Heat rose in her chest at the memory of their kiss in the forest and how safe she had felt in his arms. How for a moment he had been the Garrick she had known long ago. But now she could see that man of before was buried in regret and shame that she could not free him from.

She willed the sadness back and focused on the dark, looming presence in the distance that was Blackmore. The expansive structure signalled safety as well as the end of her time with Garrick. She'd also have to stop putting off the inevitable: facing Father's deception about her engagement; getting clarity on what role Stephen might or might not have had in the attack on her carriage; and whether she still wished to marry the man at all. One thing was for certain: she'd get the truth and the answers she deserved before she married *any* man.

Despite Garrick's desire to slow time and make this last ride with Brenna last, the distance closed swiftly. He memorised the feel of her wisps of dark hair skimming his cheek, and the soft sway of her hips back against his own as Montgomerie galloped along the open snowy meadows, so he could conjure it up on another day when he needed to remember his purpose and what happiness had once been. This was to be the end of their time together. Never again would they be this close, riding as one along the Highlands. While he had given her up as a love match in his mind, it would be hard to let her go, and the idea of never seeing her again made him shiver against her.

Time was measured from the moment before she'd entered his life and after. Perhaps the moment she left him for good and rode off with her future husband would mark yet another. Although, he couldn't fathom being there to watch her go. Winters was not that strong or good of a man.

Garrick would ensure that whatever man it was was worthy, and at present Mr Winters wasn't that. Perhaps Rory and his uncle could make a few enquiries about the man. If he lived and worked in Oban, even if only part of the year, then he would be known. If he was innocent, which seemed doubtful, and Brenna still wished to marry him, then he would support her in such, even if it turned his stomach. He'd not be a coward and slink off at sunrise. She was best without him. As she'd said yesterday, she hated him, and he really couldn't blame her.

Most days he hated himself too.

'I will ride ahead with a few men to let Laird McKenna know to expect us,' Rolf shouted back to them.

'Aye,' Garrick answered. At least he would get to see Moira and Rory again and their wee ones. It could distract him from the inevitable: saying goodbye to Brenna. At least he'd have the chance to say goodbye to her. He'd not had that chance with many of those he had loved. He would try to do right by her and make the most of it. For once, he would be doing the right thing by someone he loved.

'Are you excited to see your sister?' he asked, extending a small olive branch of conversation. Perhaps he could help them end things as friends in the end.

'Aye,' she answered, hesitation softening her voice. 'Although I have not been to visit in a long while. I should have visited sooner.'

'It is Moira. She would never be angry with you about such. Surely you know that?'

'I do.' She shifted and toyed with the edge of her cloak. 'But that shall not stop me from shaming myself for it.'

He nodded. 'I know something about that, but do not worry. She will have only joy at seeing you. The reason for your arrival will not matter.'

'I hope you are right.'

'On this one thing, I am certain.'

Soon, the large stone drive up to the castle came into view, and bands of soldiers were at the gates. Garrick smiled at the sea of Cameron and McKenna plaids. Rory was no fool. He had his men at the main castle doors, gates and stables, ready to greet them as well as the Camerons. The Camerons might be allies, but Rory was careful to keep them in check. Garrick would have done exactly the same.

He swallowed hard. If he had a clan any more, but he did not. They were dead or scattered to the shadows of the mountains. He pulled back his shoulders and thrust the truth away for another time when he could deal with it. That time wasn't now.

As Montgomerie shifted onto the smooth stone of the drive, which was covered with deeper snow, Brenna settled back against him. He wrapped his arms about her tightly for a mere moment before letting go. One final hidden embrace. As they reached the castle doors, a young lad came up to take the reins from him.

The doors opened and Moira emerged, followed closely by another soldier. 'Brenna!' she cried out joyfully. The soldier helped her down the stairs, her belly rounded with child once more.

Garrick leaned down to Brenna's ear. 'You see? She is overjoyed at the sight of you.'

'Even if I do not truly deserve it,' Brenna whispered shakily.

He dismounted and then extended his hand. 'She has long forgotten the rift between you over her marriage with Rory. You deserve every happiness.' He cherished the warmth of her palm sliding into his and the feel of her slight weight as he helped her down from Montgomerie for the last time.

'As do you, Garrick, if you would just allow yourself to believe it.' She squeezed his hand and let go.

His heart picked up speed, pounding in his chest. Before he could respond, Moira was at their side and pulling Brenna into a tight embrace.

'I am so blessed and pleased to see you as well as Garrick.' She released Brenna and hugged Garrick. Her joy at the sight of them was contagious, and he smiled. 'We have much to catch up on but let us get you attended to. A bath and clean clothes and some food.'

She fussed over her sister like the mother she now was, and Garrick revelled in the happy turn her life had taken since he'd met her years ago. 'Garrick, Rory will be returning from the village any moment.'

'Aye,' Garrick replied. 'I will see to Montgomerie until he returns.'

'And I will steal Brenna away while I can.' She flashed a grin at Garrick and tugged Brenna along, hugging her to her side. The poor woman thought them still a love match. She would be disappointed to learn otherwise, and he was grateful not to have to be the one to provide such news.

He watched them disappear within Blackmore followed by two McKenna soldiers.

If you would allow yourself to believe it.

Brenna's words echoed in his ears, but he batted them away, even though he still couldn't loosen the tightness in his chest. *Saints be.* Words were useless things at times. They didn't change anything. Least of all his mind. Especially not when it came to her. He was doing right by her by letting her go.

Garrick followed a young lad to the large stables and took over duties for Montgomerie. The mindless task would soothe his frayed nerves and settle his spirit, as it always did. He lifted the saddlebags and plaid from Montgomerie's back and heaved it over the side of the door of the stall behind him.

Grabbing the brush to rub his stallion down after such a long ride, Garrick rolled his shoulders in an attempt to shake off his frustration and focus on the task at hand. The smooth, rhythmic strokes would help ease his mind and his temper. As the minutes passed, his heart settled into a slower cadence. As he neared the end of the task, his mind was clearer and clicking through a list of items to tend to that would ensure Brenna's safety, until they were able to get her home to Glenhaven or deliver her to Mr Winters as his bride, if she still chose to marry him.

One of the tasks included getting himself far away from here. He didn't trust himself.

'You know we have stable boys for that?'

Garrick stilled and smiled before facing his old friend, Laird Rory McKenna. He set down the brush and approached. 'I suppose I've been away too long to remember such things.' They clapped one another's shoulders in greeting before embracing.

'Glad to see you're alive. Seems we've both escaped the clutches of our supposed deaths. I have escaped a curse and you the battlefield.' Rory chuckled, a deep smile on his face.

'Perhaps the world is not yet ready to be rid of us.' Garrick smiled in return but sucked in a breath as his stitches pulled at his side.

Rory's brow furrowed and gestured to Garrick's side. 'Looks like you need tending to. I can send for a physician.'

'Nay. Just needs a good cleaning and some salve. It will heal. I'm thankful to be alive and to have got Brenna here safely.'

Rory sat down on a bale of hay and Garrick sat on one just opposite to him. He ran a hand through his hair. Exhaustion began a slow, steady advance through his body, a dull ache settling in his bones. 'How is your wife?' Garrick asked, desperate to evade any questions about Brenna.

Rory's eyes lit up as they always did when he spoke of his wife, Brenna's older sister. 'Moira is well. The twins are leading us in a merry dance, and she is expecting once more.'

Garrick chuckled, feeling Rory's joy as if it were his own. 'I am thrilled to hear it. You both deserve such blessings.'

'Thank you. Truth be told, I am blessed beyond what I deserve.'

Garrick ran his hands down his trews, his gaze dropping away.

'You are a mirror of what I once believed of myself but a few years back.'

The words cut through Garrick's fatigue, and he met his friend's gaze. 'How so?'

'I thought I had no right to love Moira or have any hope for a future. My singular goal was to sire an heir and pray that a future without me would be better for all of Clan McKenna. I was a bloody fool.'

'Your lot is not mine.' Garrick shook his head and stared at his hands. 'Everything I touch turns to ash. My entire family is dead because of me: the clan scattered about to all parts of the Highlands; my home now owned by an Englishman. All because I could not protect them. I don't want Brenna to be the next casualty in my life. I told her she is better off without me. I have nothing to offer her. Not any more.'

'You couldn't have stopped any of it,' Rory stated. 'Even if you'd been here, most likely you and Brenna would be dead now.'

'All the more reason for her to be as far from me as possible.' He scrubbed a hand down his face.

Rory chuckled. 'You and I both know that will only happen if it is what *she* wishes. Come inside. Cook will heat you a plate. Some food might help clear your head.'

'I fear it may take far more than that, but I thank you for letting us stay here until we can determine who attacked her carriage and was chasing us and why.'

'Carriage attack?' Rory's eyes widened.

'Aye. That is how I came upon Brenna. Her carriage had been attacked and she was left for dead.'

'What?'

'There is much for you to catch up on. Not all could

be relayed by messenger, as I did not know who to trust.' Garrick gave Montgomerie's nose one last rub. 'Any whiskey to pair with dinner?'

'As much as you need,' Rory answered, his brow furrowed, and questions in his narrowed gaze.

'We might need a full barrel.'

Rory chuckled. 'Let's get you tended to, bathed and meet in the study. We can talk there. Any ideas on why someone might have attacked Bran's carriage?' Rory asked as they fell in step alongside each other on the walk back to the main house.

'A few. Although it wasn't Bran's carriage that was attacked. It was that of her fiancé.'

Rory stopped in his tracks. 'Fiancé? I thought…'

'Nay, we are not promised to one another. She is engaged. And he's an Englishman to boot.'

Rory cursed and carried on. 'I cannot wait to hear how that came about.'

'As you may have guessed, it was Bran's idea.'

'And that I should have guessed.' He shook his head. 'Perhaps we should all eat before we get further into those details. Moira will be none too keen to hear it. We were both under the impression that you and Brenna were still together.'

'I am shocked she did not know. How in the world did Bran and Ewan keep such a secret from her?'

'She has been unable to travel to Glenhaven to see them, and as you well know they have always been quite reluctant to visit here at Blackmore unless they are pressed to do so.' He chuckled.

'Perhaps because her father threatened to ruin you

and your clan by claiming your elopement and marriage a sham.'

Rory shook his head. 'That and my home is a vast deal larger than Glenhaven. And, as we know, Bran is a bit competitive. He cannot even be happy for his own daughter and grandchildren to be well cared for.'

Side by side they climbed the large stone steps and entered the main hall of Blackmore. As the door closed behind them, Garrick released the first real sigh of relief afforded him in the days since he'd found Brenna unconscious in a smouldering carriage. Finally, she was protected from the men that had given them chase for days. Tomorrow would be another challenge, but for today there would be peace.

Chapter Fifteen

'May I come in?' Moira called from outside Brenna's chamber.

'Aye,' Brenna answered in a shaky breath. She was nervous to finally spill the truth she had been hiding from her sister. But it was now or never, was it not?

Her chamber door opened and Brenna faced her sister and forced a smile. Moira came to her and hugged her once more, and the tenderness of her sister's embrace brought emotion to Brenna's eyes. She squeezed her sister and pulled away, daring to hold her gaze.

'I should have tried to understand and been kinder to you when you said you wished to elope with Rory years ago,' Brenna confessed, wringing her hands. 'I didn't truly understand. Not until I was in your shoes and Father was the one trying to find *me* a match.'

Moira stilled, her eyes widening. 'What do you mean? You are promised to Garrick. You came here *with* him. You are already matched, are you not?'

She shook her head. 'Father decided I was losing my

bloom waiting for him to return. When a year passed without a word from him, I gave in to Father's suggestion to find another match, as I was certain Garrick had died. Father chose another for me, although he made me believe *I* had made such a choice, that I'd done something noble for the clan in telling him I would marry Mr Winters. That I was choosing my own path. In truth, he had made the arrangement for my hand with the man long before even mentioning him to me as a possible suitor and match.' She wiped her eyes. 'I was a fool to believe I could finally win his love and respect by doing something for the clan. That he would finally value me and see my worth.

'So, yes, I am engaged, sister—but not to Garrick.'

The colour drained from her sister's face. 'What? Who would he see as a better match?'

'An Englishman.'

Moira's mouth dropped open, and she rose from the settee. She paced the room and finally ceased and stood, staring out of the large window overlooking the cliffs and sea raging below it. She popped her hands to her hips. 'You'd think he would have learned. What a blasted fool.'

Brenna sat dumbfounded. 'Did you just call Father a fool?'

'Aye. I did. What else do you call a man who makes the same mistakes over and over and belittles his own daughters in such a way?'

Brenna chuckled. She had never heard or seen *this* Moira before. Happy. Light-hearted. Direct. Speaking her mind without a wink of fear for the outcome. Brenna rather liked her sister this way.

Moira turned and smiled at her. 'Then, we shall just have to find you a way out of it. I refuse to let you marry an Englishman when there is a perfect Scottish gentleman under this roof that adores you, and you him.'

Brenna shifted on her seat, dropping her gaze. She toyed with the edge of the ribbon on the new gown Moira had given her to wear after her bath. The feel of the cool fabric was soothing as she ran it through her fingertips.

'Nay, Moira. We are not to be. He is angry. Lost. He pushes me away at every turn. Tells me I am best without him and, now that I know he chose to stay away and allow me to believe him dead, I agree with him. He abandoned me without a word. He is not the same man, Moira, no matter how it pains me to admit. Grief has shattered him. You will see.'

Moira nodded. 'He did seem…affected when I saw him on your arrival. I am so sorry to hear of it. I am tempted to meddle, as I have long adored him and the idea of a match between you, but if you do not wish it I will bite my tongue. I will *not* be Father. You are capable of making your own match.' She gripped her hands. 'And you are worthy of love, respect and so much more, sister, no matter what Father says and does. You must believe that.'

'I am trying to.'

'Then, that is all I ask, for I know it will take time to unwind what he has done, just as it did for me.' She pulled Brenna into a side hug. 'And what of this Englishman? Tell me of him. Who has Father chosen for you and why?' Moira pulled back and lifted her brow.

Brenna sighed. 'Truth be told, I am not sure I will be attaching myself to him either, despite this arrangement Father has crafted. I have many questions that need to be answered before our engagement can move forward. The first of which is whether he tried to have me killed or not.'

'Sit, sister. You will tell me everything. *Now.*'

'It is a miracle you are alive,' Rory stated, shaking his head and taking a final bite of duck. He had clung onto Garrick's and Brenna's every word as they recounted the story of their chance reunion on the road to Westmoreland.

'Aye,' Brenna agreed. 'Now we must discover why the men attacked the carriage and why they continued to give chase even after the attack was over.'

'Brenna said you both believe it might be your fiancé, Mr Winters, himself. If that is the case, we cannot allow this sham of an engagement to continue. Father will just have to find some other way to gain the power he desires. And we will assist you in whatever way we can.' Moira squared her shoulders and met Rory's gaze.

'What?' Rory asked.

''Tis true,' Garrick replied. 'I just did not wish to speak out of turn. For Brenna's sake.'

Rory sat stunned. Garrick looked at Brenna. He didn't know she'd said as much to her sister and, knowing such, he felt relief at not having to sidestep his true concerns for her sake.

Colour rose in Brenna's cheeks, giving her face a soft glow in the candlelight as she met his gaze. His chest tightened. The dark blue of her gown matched the exact colour of her eyes, and her dark hair cascaded in loose waves along her shoulders and neck. She had always been beautiful, and tonight was no exception. His appreciation for her beauty just another thing his body would need to unlearn. She would never be his. Not any more.

Their separation was his choice and hers, and for the best for both of them, but that didn't mean he would hand her over to anyone less than worthy. At the moment, Mr Winters looked more than unworthy.

'You all need not worry for me,' she countered. 'Now that we have sent word to Stephen, I am certain he will come and put things in order and assist us in getting to the truth of it, however ugly it might be.'

Garrick squeezed the napkin in his hands. *Or lie through his bloody teeth, and then I will have to kill him.*

'And he does not know we are aware of his letters between him, Father and the elusive M, so I believe we are at an advantage.'

Rory nodded and rested his napkin on the table. 'It will add an element of surprise if we accuse him of treachery when he believes he is merely arriving to pick up his future wife.'

'As well as desperation,' Garrick added. 'We must

tread carefully. I do not know what kind of man he is, and desperate men make drastic choices.'

'Aye,' Rory agreed.

'Tell me of this Mr Winters, sister,' Moira added coolly.

'He is in shipping,' Brenna answered. 'Father met him at a celebration and the King supported the idea of the match between our families, or at least that is what Father told me. He told me the union would provide us some added protection, with all the political upheaval, and the King believed it would help to illustrate a show of unity between our people and his own.'

Moira narrowed her gaze on Brenna. 'Wait. Do you believe Father is involved in the attack in some way?'

Garrick held his tongue. He knew this was a question for only Brenna to answer.

They all looked at Brenna to continue. She dropped her gaze and ran her fingertips absently over the table cloth.

'I do not wish to believe so, but after all I read in those letters, and the deception he allowed to play out to gain my agreement, I no longer know.'

Garrick's heart twisted at the agony in her voice. He could hear the tears in her voice. He wished he could take the pain she felt at her father's betrayal from her, but he knew he couldn't. Only she could weather such a storm.

'I have only met Mr Winters a few times, so much of what I know of him is business-related, as he enjoys speaking of it.' Brenna cleared her throat and took a long sip of red wine as she steered the conversation back to her fiancé.

'No matter,' Rory added. 'Uncle Leo and I will send round some enquiries and get a fuller picture of the man before he arrives. That way we'll know more of him, whether he is innocent or guilty of inciting such actions against you and thereby your clan and us as your family. Whatever happens, you have our support.'

'And mine,' Garrick added before he could stop himself. He shifted on his chair. He cursed himself. He didn't have claim to worry over her any more. But, as with all things, unlearning his love and care for her would take time. Most likely the rest of his life. He pressed a flat palm on the table to anchor himself in that idea. He wasn't sure if he found it settling or terrifying.

'If anyone needs to stretch their legs, I will be going outside, as it is time to take the hounds out for some air since Uncle Leo is away this eve. They love the snow this time of year before it gets far too cold and windy.' Rory forced a smile and rose from the table.

'I think I will join you,' Garrick added, eager to remove himself from the room and release his frustration with some movement. 'After such a ride and hearty meal—which I am most grateful for, my lady—I could do with a walk.'

'I will not be joining you, husband,' Moira announced, 'As I am worn through.' Rory came over and kissed her cheek. 'Be sure to grab your bonnet,' she chided.

'Aye,' he answered. 'Do keep your sister out of trouble, Brenna,' he added, before Moira playfully swatted his arm.

'I will try,' Brenna answered, and smiled at her sister.

Once the men were all out of doors and far from the house, Rory broached the subject first. 'I shall send enquiries out tomorrow,' he offered. 'And adding more men to the watch outside is in order. Something seems…off about the whole business.'

'I am quite certain I don't have all of the pieces to the story of this union and the urgency of it, despite my enquiries of Brenna, because Bran misled her as well. What do you think?' Garrick flipped up the collar of his coat.

'If Bran is a part of it, I am sure you are right. But he is often reluctant to confide the truth in anyone, as you well know.' Rory nested his hands in his trews.

'Aye,' Garrick answered. 'So how shall we go about it without stirring up too much suspicion before our arrival?'

They walked in silence for a few moments as the three hounds bounded out in the snow, barking with pleasure as they skidded in the lush flakes and chased one another. The wind blew softly, sending an arc of snow in whatever direction they ran. The cool wind helped clear Garrick's head, and he began to think more clearly.

'The Camerons, as much as it pains me to say it,' Rory said flatly. 'If anyone can ferret out the truth, they can.'

'I believe you are right, but there is some tension between them and the Stewarts based on Rolf's reaction upon seeing Brenna yesterday.'

Rory nodded. 'An issue with a lame stallion and a delivery of goods months back. Man couldn't get all the way to the Camerons, so he stopped at Glenhaven for aid. Bran provided aid but claimed the stallion and goods as his own for his good deed.'

'Sounds about right.' Garrick shook his head.

'It's worse than you think. He is not well. I have noticed it in his rambling correspondence. I believe it is from the stroke.' Rory's brow furrowed.

'Have you spoken to Moira of it? Brenna made a brief mention of him being different, but she wasn't terribly forthcoming with details.'

'I cannot quite find the words. Bran and I never started on solid footing with one another, as you well know, so I have always been careful about sounding too harsh or doing anything to sever what tenuous connection with him we do have. He is Moira's father, after all. But, if he is ill, it may be why he was in such a rush to secure this union for Brenna without much thought to the consequences of her happiness, or really investigating the man before committing her to him.'

'But surely Ewan has some investment in this outcome and the implications of such a union? He is her brother and in line to become laird.' Garrick kicked a tuft of snow.

Rory nested his hands in the pockets of his coat. 'I believe he is trying, but he is out of his depth trying to guide Bran and the clan with all that has happened in the Highlands over the last year. Uprisings, poor crops and small bands of reivers popping up along the borderlands as well as in the middle of the Highlands. Much has changed since you have been away.'

Garrick stared out into the snowy twilight and the midnight-blue sky settled into his bones.

'We have offered aid to Ewan as well as Bran, but they rebuff us at every turn. I believe it may be due to our new alliance with the Camerons.' Rory shrugged. 'The man has the pride of his father. He is a Stewart through and through.'

'Where does that leave us, then?'

'Enquiries about Winters and a complete recounting of what happened since you discovered Brenna,' Rory answered. 'We'll meet in the study tomorrow morn and see if we can work this through after you've had a good night's sleep. Between all of us, we should be able to come to the truth of it.'

'And Brenna and Moira?'

Rory smiled. 'I am sure they're plotting as well as we speak. They are also Stewarts, as you well know. They will not sit by and let us work this out alone. Moira will come to me when she is ready with her plan.' He smiled and chuckled. 'She always does.'

An unexpected spike of jealousy rippled through Garrick. How he longed for a relationship such as Rory's and Moira's. Or at least, he used to. He was not worthy of one now. He was too broken to be able to offer much to anyone, let alone a woman such as Brenna. But it did not mean some small seed of hope within him did not still long for it, and see what Rory had as the treasure he'd once believed he might also have, and feel morose at what he had forsaken.

It is for the best. She deserves better.

And, by God, he would make sure she got the best. He would make sure this Mr Winters was not the cad his gut told him he was. If Bran had made another horrid match for his youngest daughter, Garrick would expose the truth and set Brenna free from it before it became official and binding, so she could make a better and more suitable match with another man who would secure her future. She would not suffer as Moira had from her first arranged marriage.

Garrick would die first.

Chapter Sixteen

Despite being clean with a full belly, and resting on the softest of beds, Brenna had a fitful night of sleep. She woke to sunlight streaming in her room across her feet and the dreaded feeling that she was missing something of import. She bolted up, scanned the room and then flopped back down as her stomach flipped at the realisation. She was missing someone, not something: *Garrick.*

It was the first morning she had not woken to the sight of his unshaven face above her, or the husky burr of his voice at her ear, and the absence unsettled her. 'Why can you not let him go?' she muttered to herself, shielding her eyes with her forearm. She was being a lovesick fool, and she wouldn't stand for it. They'd made their decisions to be apart for the sake of one another, hadn't they? Today needed to be the first day to her moving on with the rest of her life.

Perhaps she could marry and revel in the thrill of motherhood as Moira had. Her stomach clenched in unease. But to whom? Despite being engaged, she was uncertain of her future, as Stephen Winters' intentions were foggy at best and deadly at worst. She nibbled her lip. Could he be innocent somehow? Could the letters, coin and pursuers be some bizarre conspiracy to make him appear guilty? She rolled her eyes at her own ridiculousness.

Why on earth would anyone go to such trouble to make a man look guilty? The simple answer was that they wouldn't. Odds were Stephen was involved somehow, as some of the letters were from him, and the coin as well. Despite wanting to believe her romantic history was less horrid than her first love abandoning her and the second man, her fiancé, trying to *kill* her, she couldn't quite shake the possibility. Blast. How had her love life turned into a romantic saga? She ran her hands through her mussed hair. Maybe Ayleen had had the right idea by heading to the abbey to devote her life to something bigger than herself and away from men and their scheming.

She sighed. But Ayleen had had an even worse end, hadn't she? Brenna stared out of the large, expansive window that showcased the sea just beyond the cliffs. Its still, dark waters calmed her, and she watched until her heart slowed and her mind cleared. Her grief over losing Garrick had made her wilfully choose something just to please Father, but this was her life, and she needed to start trusting her own mind and making her own decisions, no matter the consequences. She threw back her covers and decided to take charge of what remained of her messy life. She was not married yet, was she?

She would dress, break her fast and take charge of her future. If the men were planning enquiries into Stephen's dealings anyway, she would make enquiries of her own. She'd ask Garrick to see again those letters they had found on one of their attackers, so she was prepared for her meeting with him. Now that he knew she was here, he would come for her, otherwise how would it look?

He'd look guilty without even trying. It was only a matter of when he would arrive. Today? Tomorrow? The day after? She needed to make the most of the time she had.

After breaking her fast, Brenna went to the study, where she found Garrick and Rory sitting in silence, poring over maps and correspondence.

'Good morn,' Rory offered as she crossed the threshold of his study.

The tables were filled with letters, ledgers and books, and the smell of the fire, leather and books filled her nose. She smiled. It reminded her of her father's study. 'Good morn,' she said. 'May I see those letters we found on the person of that man chasing us?' Brenna stood before them at the study door.

Garrick nodded. 'Aye. We've looked them over. Didn't see anything new of real import since we still don't know who M is.' He rose from the large chair he sat in, gathered the letters from Rory's desk and handed them to her. 'What do you hope to find?'

She avoided his gaze and took the letters near to the

hearth, so she could keep warm and be as physically far away from Garrick as she could. He smelled of clean soap and spice, and she abhorred the humming it sent along her limbs. 'I am not entirely sure, but I want to know everything I can about these letters before Mr Winters arrives. I plan to interrogate him until we arrive at the truth of what happened and why, no matter how ugly it might be.'

And ugly it might be. She prayed Father wasn't involved but a tiny whispering along her mind warned her that he might be. And, if he had been, she hoped it was not intended, but merely a consequence he had not foreseen.

'A fine idea. Enquiries have been sent out by messenger to the Camerons and some business contacts I have in Oban. I also sent word to Mr Winters as well as your father so they would be aware of what happened, as well of your safe arrival here. I also took the liberty of inviting Mr Winters to Blackmore to get better acquainted.'

A muscle worked in Garrick's jaw. 'That's one way of putting it,' he muttered.

Brenna bit her lip. While she wished to know more about Mr Winters, she was unsure of what they would find. She also worried over what Father would think of their enquiries. He never responded well to any challenge to his decisions. And despite all she still wanted him to be proud of her just once, especially if he had but little time left.

She steeled her spine and pushed away Old Brenna, or at least she attempted to. She couldn't care for her own safety *and* protect Father's feelings at the same time. It was time she put herself first in her own future, even if that meant he might never really be proud of her as she had long hoped.

'Thank you,' she replied, lifting her chin. 'I appreciate your thoroughness on the matter. I think we are all quite eager to see what those enquiries yield.'

Garrick narrowed his gaze at her, confusion written all over his furrowed brow. She smiled at him, snuggled deep into the oversized chair, flipped open the first letter and began to read, forcing the uncertainty and worry out of her mind. If she was to shed Old Brenna's insecurities, she had to be more convincing, starting now.

Garrick recognised the hesitation in Brenna's voice. It did not matter how finely she tried to mask it with her words. She was scared, nervous about trying to exert some control over her future, and he understood what an undertaking it was. Lairds were not used to being challenged and thwarted. Power bent to them and they expected their families to do the same, especially their children. 'Do not worry about your father,' he offered. 'If there is an issue, we will intervene on your behalf.'

'Perhaps I do not want you to intervene,' she stated, scanning the first letter.

'I think I shall get some more tea,' Rory said and stepped out, closing the door behind him.

Evidently, Rory knew when to abandon ship. Garrick was too stubborn to care. He was trying to help ensure a good future for Brenna and help her avoid the pitfalls he'd had with his own father. Didn't she see that?

'Why do you resist my efforts to help you at every turn?' he asked.

'Says the person who resisted my every effort to help you.'

He looked heavenward. 'We are talking of two entirely different situations, and you know it. I was helping us stay alive. I could not allow you to put your life in danger.'

'Do you not have other matters of your own to tend to?' She continued speaking with her back to him.

He frowned and approached where she sat by the hearth, reading the letters. 'Of course I do, but I cannot just leave you here without knowing who was after you and whether this Mr Winters will protect you. If he is worthy of you.'

'I will be well here with Rory, Moira and the hounds to look after me. Your task is complete, Garrick Mac-Lean. I arrived here safely. You should go.'

'Go? You must be joking. I risked my life to get you here. I will see this through.'

'Even if I do not want you to?'

Ire flared up in his gut. 'Should I have left you there in that burning carriage? Or perhaps allowed you to be killed and drowned in that stream by some English brute?' He gripped her by the arm and turned her to face him.

'As I said before. I want you to go and to never see you again.' Her eyes were bright in the firelight, too bright. Wild and uncertain, like an animal snared.

'That is not what you said to me two nights ago when you kissed the breath out of me,' he said, his words low, husky and dripping with intention. 'Have you so soon forgotten?'

Her breathing faltered and a pulse throbbed at the side of her throat. Nay. She had not forgotten. Her lips parted involuntarily.

'Nay. And if I remember, you kissed me as well,' she murmured, shifting away from the fire and out of his hold.

'Then let me make sure the man who will kiss those lips for the rest of your days is worthy of it.'

She swallowed hard. 'So be it. Do as you will, and I will do as I must.'

'I will,' he answered, taking a step away from her.

Minutes ticked by on the clock on the mantel, and Garrick willed his temper to settle and his worry over her to abate. His emotion and fear were driving his words, and such rashness wouldn't solve anything. Brenna stood staring off into the distance out of the large windows. He steadied himself. 'In order to get to the truth, we need to work together. And the only way to do that is for you to be completely honest with me. Did anyone else know you would be returning that day? Had Winters sent word to anyone else to let them know of your plans to travel?'

She didn't answer at first, and he wasn't sure if she was ignoring him or shutting him out. Then, she nodded. 'Aye. He had notified his mother, who lives in town with his sister, as well as his staff at his estate, and his business partner. But, like I said, he had planned to join us and was called away at the very last moment. If someone was waiting for him in the carriage on our way to Glenhaven, then why did they chase *us*?'

'I don't know, but the one man seemed focused on separating us and harming you.' He shook his head. 'And your father's enemies? Did any of them know?'

'His enemies are vast, as you well know. Some might have been aware of my visit, as Father was touting it about that he was doing this to please the King, and all of the extra privileges he expected to receive because of it, but I can't imagine they would have known of my early departure. Unless they were watching Stephen's residence.' Colour rose in her cheeks and she crossed her arms against her chest.

Garrick's recognised the shame burning her face and adding red blotches along her neckline. He pressed his lips together and offered what little he could: his own truth. 'You do not need to be ashamed of his scheming or your ignorance of his manipulation of your future. My father was the same. It seems they had that in common as a tactic to keep their children in line.'

Her shoulders sagged forward and she ran her fingertips along the edge of her plait. 'Moira has strong, unwavering devotion to her interests in books and botany, and Ewan is dedicated to leading the clan and learning the ways of laird. I suppose I should merely resign myself that I will never please Father, as I am neither. I have tried and tried to gain his approval, but I am always lacking. I am not witty, useful or talented enough, I suppose.' She smirked. '"Thank God, you're pretty, Bren," he used to say. "Not much else to be had."'

Garrick stilled. The words slammed against his chest with force, the intent cutting him. While he knew Bran had been a thoughtless and controlling man at times, Garrick didn't know how cruel he had been to her. So many things she'd said and done over the time he had known her made sense, the pieces of her he didn't understand clicking into place. She had been so pleasing to survive, so yielding to attempt to gain favour, and so gentle and encouraging of him because she knew what it felt like to have neither from someone she loved.

'I am just blown about with the wind,' she continued. 'I do not know what interests me other than fashion and that seems ridiculous at best. My value seems tied to whom I can marry and, when I believed I could choose a match to finally earn his respect and pride, I jumped at the chance.' She let go of the end of her plait of hair. 'Like a fool. I did not know there was no choice in it as it had already been decided for me.'

Garrick fisted his hands by his sides and chose his words with care. 'Bren, you have immense value and purpose in your own right, untethered from any man. Your worth is beyond what any man thinks of you. Not me, your father or your brother. It is within what you believe of yourself.'

While he knew all of these things to be true, he also knew how hard it was to apply it to one's own life, for he struggled to remember his own worth. He felt hypocritical to say so as he could not follow his own advice, but he had to try.

'You do not understand. You are a man. A soldier. A laird. You are respected and valued for your contributions and skills. I am…invisible.' She gazed at the tips of her shoes.

Garrick came to her and paused, hesitating at closing the remaining distance between them. Did he dare? He took one of her hands in his own, the small, fragile weight of it sliding against his flesh making him feel light-headed. The familiar friction was like tinder. He had to take care he didn't catch flame.

'Perhaps I do not fully understand,' he began. 'But I do know how words can damage a child.'

She did not move away from his hold but met his gaze instead. 'Do you?'

He nodded. 'After my brother died, my father used to tell me how he wished it had been me or Cairn that had died in Lon's place, daily for quite some time. I know it was grief, but it pained us all the same, as we were grieving too. And, despite all I tried, I could never win his approval. After a time, I gave up entirely.'

She sucked in a breath and squeezed his hand. 'I am glad it was not you that died that day, and I am so sorry you had to hear those words from your father. You did not deserve them.'

'Nor did you deserve such words from yours.'

'So, how did you overcome that sadness after your father died? Of knowing he wasn't proud of you?'

'I realised he could not love me and respect me as I wished him to. He wasn't capable of it for reasons beyond my control, and I would never understand why. I had to decide to accept the man he was for all of his frailties as my father or let him go entirely. I could never find any middle ground.'

'And what did you do?'

'Honestly? Something in between those two.'

She chuckled.

Rory came back into the room quietly, carrying a cup of tea, and Moira followed closely behind.

Brenna squeezed Garrick's hand and let go. 'Thank you for your advice. I will try,' she answered gently.

'Any progress?' Moira asked, her gaze flitting between them as she pulled her shawl tightly around her shoulders.

'Unfortunately, none. We cannot discern the purpose of the attack, nor the reason for the chase afterwards. If they were seeking Winters, he wasn't there, and Arthur, Roland and Brenna should have been spared. And if they were seeking Brenna, and she was the intended victim, then why?' said Garrick.

'We've received word from the note we sent by messenger to Winters last night,' Rory offered. His frown warned Garrick he wouldn't like the news.

'Your Mr Winters is thrilled to hear of your safe arrival and he will be here tomorrow to collect you and bring you to Oban for your nuptials.' He cleared his throat. 'Seems your father has approved a union as soon as possible due to the unsavoury events. He wishes you to be settled as quickly as possible.'

Brenna paled and sunk back in the large chair by the fire. 'Tomorrow?'

Chapter Seventeen

Brenna's heart hammered in her chest. *Tomorrow?* She swallowed hard. For all her talk of wanting to exert control over her life, her stomach lurched at the thought of facing Stephen Winters. Getting to the truth of what had happened would be ugly and dangerous. Who knew what he might do when he realised they suspected him of treachery?

She gripped the arm of the chair, grateful it offered some support as her legs felt like they might buckle from beneath her if she'd been standing. 'How shall we go about getting to the truth?'

'Carefully,' Rory answered, handing her the letter. 'He knows of the attack and will know something is afoot, especially if he intended…' He stopped himself.

She sighed. 'Me dead. I know.'

Moira came over and pressed a hand to her shoulder. 'We are with you. You are not alone. No harm will come to you. You have my word.'

'Do you think Father truly agreed to moving the

wedding forward or might Stephen be making it up?' Even after all that had happened with Father, she didn't wish to believe he would be so eager to give her to a man who might be wishing her dead.

Moira didn't answer but squeezed her shoulder, which was answer enough.

Thistles. Why had she even asked?

'Your father may not have put together that Stephen is behind the attack and thinking that you might be safer with a husband,' Garrick offered. 'Or he may be desperate and not thinking clearly due to his illness.'

She squirmed in the chair. The wave of uncertainty that always accompanied her feelings of trying to please her father washed over her, leaving her chilled and confused. One crisis at a time, she reminded herself. She'd deal with Stephen tomorrow and then perhaps Father the next. Either way, she would be seeing Mr Winters in less than a day and she didn't feel the least bit prepared. Perhaps, if she focused on only getting to the truth behind the attacks, she could muster the courage to face whatever fruits it revealed.

'What is our plan?' she asked, eager to do rather than worry. 'If I do nothing, I will go mad before he arrives. What can I do?'

'Perhaps you can discern a timeline of the letters. Most are dated. It may help us see when the exchange began and when the most recent ones were sent.' Garrick gave her a stack of the letters. 'Then we can compile some questions that may help us glean what role he had in all of this.'

She took the letters from him. 'And the responses from your contacts? And the Camerons?'

Rory shook his head. 'I think it will be too soon to receive word back from all of them, but I hope we will have received a few prior to Mr Winters' arrival.'

She hoped so too.

'I will help you write out the timing of events,' Moira offered. After gathering a large parchment, quill and ink, she set them on the large table. After drawing out a large line, she added check marks. 'Once you organise them, tell me the start and end date and then we can plot in the exchanges as we can. Surely knowing the sequence of events shall help us glean their purpose.'

'Let us hope you are right, sister.'

Brenna set the letters out along the line one by one, moving the letters as needed when newer or later dated letters emerged. After she placed the last one, she frowned.

'What is it?' Moira asked, looking over Brenna's shoulder at the timeline now dotted with letters.

'I cannot place it, but there is something not right about this timing. There is a tight clump of letters here, then a huge gap in time without any communications, and then another bunch at the end. I believe we are missing those.' She pointed to the void on the parchment.

Moira stilled. 'Is that not when Father was ill?'

Brenna looked at the gap. 'Aye. It is. You are right!'

'But someone still managed all of his correspondence. Who was it?'

'Not Ewan,' Brenna replied. 'He detests letter writing. One of the many things he will have to overcome once he is laird.'

Garrick and Rory looked up at them both. 'So, who assisted him with that when he was ill?' Rory asked. 'It would have had to be one of his most trusted men.'

Brenna shrugged. 'They were many of the leading clansmen in and out of his chambers at all hours, and I was in such a state, I cannot say with certainty if one man had more visits with him than others. Ewan might know…but by the time we get word to him and back, it will be too late. Winters arrives tomorrow.'

'Could you compile a list?' Moira asked. 'Even if it might be incomplete?'

'Of course.' She added the names of five of Father's top leaders within the clan.

Adam
Stephens
Callum
Hamilton
Alistair

None of them had a name starting with *M*. She frowned. So much for that idea.

'Could one of them have interceded in the discourse? Could they have a batch of the letters?' Garrick asked.

'Possibly. But to what end?' Brenna asked.

'A great question,' Rory answered.

'What if Father has nothing to do with this? What if Winters has nothing to do with us?'

The three of them gifted Brenna a droll look.

'I was just being hopeful,' she murmured. 'You cannot be cross with me wishing my fiancé and Father were not part of some bizarre conspiracy to kill me.'

'Nay. None of us fault you in that. I suppose we just wish to prepare you in case they are,' Garrick added. 'What is the timeline you have?'

''Tis a year in length from November of last year to this November with a gap of about four months long between last March to July. Then, the letters begin again.' Brenna studied it. 'And the break mirrors the time of Father's illness, but other than that I do not know of its import.' She rubbed her temple. There had to be something she was missing.

When she glanced up, she caught Garrick's gaze on her. Questions registered in his eyes, and something else entirely that made her body quake from within. She swallowed hard. Perhaps he had just realised what she had.

That, despite her efforts at distance, the thing she was truly missing was him.

'I think I shall take some air. My temples throb,' Brenna stated and set aside the parchment.

Moira began to follow, but Garrick touched her arm. 'Let me go. Please.'

She smiled and nodded to him. 'I think you know where you will find her.'

'Aye,' he answered and nodded. Brenna always went to the barn when she was worried or upset. Countless times, they had spent lazy afternoons lying on bales talking...or kissing. His blood warmed and pooled at the memories. The burst of cold air on his face as he exited the castle cooled him and helped him regain his focus. When he entered the barn and saw her leaning her head against Montgomerie's, her eyes closed as she ran her fingertips along his neck and murmuring to him, he faltered.

How would he ever let her go? He swallowed hard. His mission was to put her mind at ease and to let her know all would be well. As a friend, which he desperately still wished to be, he needed to do this for her. Freeing her of his own weakness was best for her, but he had to help her to do that. He needed to let her go by explaining himself, truly explaining himself.

'I need to tell you why I never returned for you. Why I never wrote.'

Her hand stilled along Montgomerie's neck and her eyes fluttered open before she lifted her head to face him. Her brow furrowed. 'Did you not already tell me? You said it was grief after Ayleen died. You could not face returning. Was there more?'

He reached out his hand to her, and she slipped it in his own hesitantly. Garrick's heart thundered in his chest, heat flushed his body and for a moment he wasn't sure if his boots touched the ground. The only thing anchoring him to this moment was the weight of her hand in his and the warmth of it radiating up his arm.

After they sat on two bales of hay facing one another, he let go of her hand. She smoothed her skirts and cloak with her hands and then linked them together loosely in her lap. Could he do this? His throat dried and he scrubbed a hand through his hair.

When he met her gaze, he knew he had to explain so she would believe in herself, in her worth and in her value and know that she need not settle for any man. Not him, Winters, or any man lacking. She had to know she was worthy of all the world had to offer, not merely what Bran told her she was.

'You are, you were, the most beautiful gift I have ever been given, Bren.'

'Garrick—'

'Nay,' he said softly. 'Please let me say all of it. Just listen.'

She nodded, pressing her lips together in a smooth line.

'I did not write, I could not write, to you after Ayleen died…' His hands shook and he blew out a breath and held her gaze. 'Because I killed her.'

Her lips parted, her eyes searching his face. She shifted on the bale. No judgement rested in her eyes only a quest for understanding, so he continued on despite how his hands and limbs tingled and buzzed.

'I arrived in time at the abbey. It was engulfed in flames and reivers were everywhere, attacking the area and everyone within sight as they pillaged the abbey and whatever remained of the cottages nearby on the outskirts of Perth. I prayed to God to find her, and I heard this scream.' He cleared his throat as the ache of emotion tightened it.

Brenna shifted forward at the edge of the bale.

'I saw her. She saw me. The reivers were closing in. I was there in time but still could not save her because

I froze. I could have run to her and rescued her, but I did nothing, as if my legs were roots in the ground.'

A flash of heat consumed his body and illness threatened, but he swallowed it back. 'And, because I froze and did not act, she died. I saw the disappointment and disbelief in her eyes when she met my gaze and I didn't move. And, when the reiver stabbed her, the agony...' He choked back a sob. 'By the time I did finally run to her and reached her, she was dead. And *I*... I killed her.'

He looked away, staring at the barn floor as the world blurred from the emotion filling his eyes. Shame bled out of him. His fingers tingled, his heart pounded in his chest and his body heated at the acknowledgement of all his weakness had caused. He'd never admitted all that had happened with Ayleen to anyone before. Saying it out loud felt as horrid as it was freeing. At least one other person in the world knew his full shame, all of it, not just the filtered parts he had shown to her.

'And, because I failed her so completely, I could not allow myself to be your husband, Bren. I did not deserve it. The idea of failing you was more of a risk than I could take. So, I abandoned you, not because you were not worthy, but because *I* was not worthy of you and your love. I let you go...in order to save you from myself.'

'Garrick,' Brenna murmured. She sat down beside him on the bale of hay, resting her palm against the side of her face. The lovely, warm feel of comfort was his undoing, and the emotion he had fought to keep at bay burst free and he sobbed.

Ayleen. Cairn. Mother. All dead because of me.

Ack. Why did he have to be so bloody weak?

'Please look at me,' she whispered. She leaned over and clutched his face within her hands, her thumbs wiping the tears from his cheeks that he hadn't even realised were falling.

He clutched her wrists and shook his head. He couldn't meet her gaze. He didn't dare. He couldn't show her his weakness any more. He hated himself enough already. If she did, he wouldn't be able to breathe.

She let go and kneeled before him, forcing him to look into her eyes. The clear, blue depths of her eyes held no judgement or censure but…love. The way she used to look at him. As if he was the best of men. As if he could conquer the world with a flick of his wrist. He sucked in a breath. Did he scarce believe that she would forgive him for what he'd done?

'I am so sorry,' he murmured, clutching her face. 'I never meant to—'

Her gaze dropped to his lips and it was his undoing. He pulled her to him roughly, kissing her urgently, desperately, as if she was his breath that he needed to survive. Her breath caught in surprise, but she didn't pull back. She leaned into him, wrapping her legs around his waist as he pressed her tightly against him. Deepening kiss after kiss, he held her, knowing he should stop, but his body refused to obey his command. She felt like water after a drought, sun after a flood. She was all he needed, and yet nothing he felt he could still ask for.

He clutched her thigh, savouring the solid strength of her body, craving a union with her.

Ayleen.

If he didn't stop, he would compromise Brenna's very future. He pulled back, knowing full well he shouldn't have kissed her. That, even now he had finally told her the full truth of what had happened to Ayleen and why he'd chosen to abandon her, he still didn't deserve her.

Running a hand down her cheek, he pressed his forehead to her own, listening to the cadence of their uneven breaths. 'I still do not deserve you, but I wanted you to know that it was never you that was unworthy, but me. Wait for the man who deserves you, Bren. Choose your future. Do not allow any man to do it for you.'

Chapter Eighteen

Brenna shivered in Garrick's hold. His kisses, his touch, his hold affected her even more so than it always had. Her body thrummed and ached with desire. She sucked in steadying breaths and closed her eyes, breathing in his scent of soap and spice, knowing full well that she could not leave him, but knowing she had to all the same.

His telling her the truth behind his abandonment had set them both free, but it did not heal the scars of the past. They were still there alive and well, separating them. He couldn't forgive himself for what had happened to Ayleen and his family, and she didn't know if he ever could. And how could she live a life with a man who held his shame over the past closer than his hopes for the future?

She leaned in against his cheek and kissed him one last time. 'I will always love you, Garrick MacLean. You are the best of men and always will be. I hope one day you will remember that.'

She extricated herself carefully from his hold, her legs trembling as they made contact with the ground, and slipped away without a word before she changed her mind. His words had helped her realise that only she could free herself and secure her own happiness and, like her sister Moira, she would do just that.

But she'd have to hurry to set such a plan in motion as her fiancé would arrive on the morrow. As she walked back to the castle, the foundation of her plan began to shape before her. It was midday, but she would have enough time to craft her trap.

She entered the castle, went in search of her sister and found her in the massive Blackmore library and sitting room Rory had set up for his wife, poring over old ledgers.

'What are you looking for?' Brenna asked as she crossed the threshold into the room, basking in the warmth of the roaring fire and heady smell of leather and must.

Moira glanced up from the scattered books and smiled at her, attempting to rise.

'Do not get up. I will come to you. I wish to ask you a favour after all.'

Moira tilted her head, quirking her lips as she scrutinised her sister. 'What exactly are you up to? There is an unnatural twinkle in your eyes.'

'I am merely taking a page from my eldest sister's doings and seizing my right to make my own match.' She gleamed, and Moira clapped her hands together.

'You and Garrick have mended your rift and your engagement to Winters is off! I am so relieved.'

Brenna sat at the table with her. 'Nay, sister. Although we have mended many of our differences, we are not engaged. Nor have I ended my arrangement with Mr Winters. But I do wish to enlist your help in preparing for my meeting with him tomorrow. Can you help?'

Moira's smile fell. 'Aye. Of course, you can count on me. What can I do?'

'I will need you to craft a letter in Father's hand and secure a seal to it to make it look as if it is from Father. As you did when you planned your elopement with Rory.'

'First of all, I did not forge a letter from Father, but merely the seal to escape detection when Rory and I were scheming my escape.' She lifted her nose a touch to emphasise her point.

Brenna rolled her eyes. 'Either way, can you do this for me? I will draft what I would like you to put in it. Then, if you will copy it and seal it.' She shifted on the seat. 'And then if you could ask Rory to present it to him as if it is from Father.' She smiled.

'He will only do so if you tell him why.'

'I wish to attempt to make Winters reveal more of his hand if he is involved in this plot to harm me and our family. If he is innocent, he will be nonplussed by the letter from Father.'

'You mean the fake letter from Father?'

'Aye, the fake letter from Father.' She gifted her sister a full smile. 'So, will you do it?'

'Aye,' she answered, grasping Brenna's hand in her own. 'Draft what you wish me to write and I shall begin.'

* * *

Garrick rubbed his eyes. 'The words are beginning to swim upon the page,' he complained, and glanced over to Rory, who was also immersed in correspondence.

'At least we have heard back from some of our queries,' Rory replied.

'Too bad most of it contradicts one another.'

'It is odd. I have never seen such opposing views of a man. Some of Uncle's contacts claim he is a fine businessman while others that he is a debtor and just short of a criminal.' Rory set the pages down and leaned back in his chair.

Garrick stood to stretch and then walked over to the large window. 'Looks like rain.'

'Most likely it will be snow. Temperature is falling.'

'Aye.' He stared out at the rolling sea, the smooth waves reminding him of the feel of Brenna against him. His body began a dull hum and his palms ached to hold her.

'Do you plan to just let her go tomorrow?' Rory asked. The words cut through the air like an arrow and Garrick's heart sputtered as if it had hit its mark.

He sighed aloud and let his head flop forward momentarily before he looked back up. 'Aye. I do not wish to, but I am not the man she deserves. I want her to choose the best man and future for herself. That is not me. I am broken, and I literally have nothing to offer her. Not even a roof over her head or a bed to sleep in.' He released a bitter laugh. 'I am laird over a clan that

no longer exists, and a man without a home or castle.'
He rested his hands on his waist.

'If I am any example, Stewart women like their men
a wee bit broken. Look at me. I was cursed and dying
when Moira chose me and agreed to become my wife.
I did not deserve her in the least, but she is the best gift
I have ever been given. Because of her, I have a life, a
family and a future. She fought for my life and well-
being when I had stopped fighting for it myself. Seizing the chance you gifted me was the best decision I
have ever made, even though I was certain I had made
a fatal error at the time.'

'You and Moira are different. 'Tis not the same with
Bren and me.'

'No? Seems exactly the same to me, but you are a
mite bit more stubborn than I am.' Rory chuckled at
his own joke and set back to reading his correspondence. 'Have you located anyone who might be the M
from the letters?'

Garrick shook his head. 'Unfortunately, no.' He
glanced back at the two letters that remained unopened
on the table. 'But I have two more to read. Let us hope
one of them is the hidden piece of the puzzle we seek.'
He set aside his longings for Brenna and went back
to read the remaining letters. 'While there is no mention of who M might be, these two letters speak of the
suspicion that Winters has been earning favour from
both sides of the coin. Perhaps that is why some speak
favourably while others do not. They suggest he is in
league with the King while also trying to show alle-
giance to a few of the southern clans.'

Rory whistled.

'What?' Garrick asked, eager to know what his friend was thinking.

'Think upon it,' Rory urged, sitting forward in his chair, his palms pressed flat to his desk. 'If that is true, then he very well may be the fiend we believe he is. It might also explain why he might be eager to create a rift between the two sides. And what better way to do that than to murder the daughter of a laird that was set upon marrying an Englishman? Everyone would be engulfed in anger and no one would win. All sides would be at odds.'

'That would set England and Scotland at odds with one another. And you are right, everyone would be enraged. The Scots for the death of a laird's daughter and the English for a man losing his betrothed.'

The hall clock chimed six. 'Let us meet to dine at seven and tell Moira and Brenna our theory. From there, we can determine the best way to ensnare Mr Winters for the rat we believe him to be.'

Garrick nodded, but he balked at the idea of how they might go about it. He couldn't think of a way of entrapping the man without using Brenna as bait, and he was none too keen to do so. Desperate men were dangerous creatures, especially if they were as cunning as Mr Winters seemed to be. Not just anyone could fool both sides into believing in his loyalty. Only a man gifted in deceit could weave a bevy of lies into a tapestry, and he feared Winters might be capable of such treachery.

Chapter Nineteen

Brenna took a steadying breath and pulled back her shoulders before rounding the corner and entering the long main hallway of Blackmore. Each step along the stone corridor was a reminder of who she walked towards and why. This was her chance to get the answers she needed, and she would get them no matter what. Her smile fell away when she saw the man before her.

'Where is Stephen… Mr Winters?' she asked, befuddled to see a man other than her betrothed at the door, handing off his coat and gloves to the young maid who had greeted him.

'Do not worry, darling,' Stephen called as he entered through the expansive doors of the castle. 'I am here. I am relieved to see you looking so well.' Stephen came to her, gathered her hands in his own and smiled, pressing a kiss to her knuckles.

What had come over him? While this *looked* like the Stephen Winters she had meet in Oban during her visits, he had never been this attentive and affectionate before. Maybe he did care for her, but he had been more reserved before their betrothal had been made official. Had almost losing her thrust him into being a more doting fiancé?

Did it matter?

Brenna hesitated before gifting him a full smile. 'I have Laird MacLean to thank.' She gestured to Garrick, who frowned at Stephen. She nodded to him, her eyes pleading for him to be kind. Their ruse would not work if he was too sceptical of the man.

'I am indebted to you, my laird.' He nodded to Garrick. 'I hope to one day be able to repay you for your bravery in rescuing my bride-to-be.'

Garrick cleared his throat and stood in a soldier's stance with his feet apart and his hands linked behind his back. 'You can start by explaining why you did not send her with more protection.'

Brenna's throat dried. So much for subtleties.

He shrugged. 'Ignorance of the ways of these lands. I did not think it would be such a risk, and with my plans changing at the last minute I could not find more men to send with them. I was trying to please her by getting her back home that night, as she wished. It is a mistake I will not repeat, I assure you.' He pulled Brenna to his side and kissed the top of her head. 'I am so grateful you came along when you did.'

Garrick shifted on his feet. 'As am I.'

The meaning of his words was not lost on her, and she blushed.

'Welcome to Blackmore, Mr Winters,' Moira said. 'Please come in. We would love you to stay for dinner, if you can. We would like to get to know our future brother-in-law.'

'Such a generous offer, my lady. I wish we could stay. I would like to get us home and settled by dark to avoid any further danger to Miss Stewart. With our nuptials only a handful of days away, we cannot tarry, even if we wish to. But I would not shy away from a refreshment before we depart. Perhaps tea?'

'Of course. I'll see to it. I am glad you can stay for a visit, even if it is a brief one.'

Brenna exhaled in relief as they moved into the main hall. So far, so good.

'Thank you for welcoming me into your home, Laird McKenna, and for your correspondence about Miss Stewart. I was sick with worry when we heard the carriage had not arrived at Glenhaven as planned.'

'As were we, Mr Winters. Correspondence from Laird Stewart arrived for you as well.' He handed him the note.

'Ah, thank you,' he answered. A slight hesitation in his reply was his only flicker of uncertainty. He tucked the letter in his jacket pocket.

'Do you not wish to read it now?' Brenna asked, hoping she didn't sound as eager as she felt. He needed to read the note for her to know whether he was involved in the plot against her. 'It could be about our nuptials and whether Father will be well enough to join us.'

He smiled at her. 'Quite right. I will scan it to see if there is anything to be shared.' He opened the seal and read. His smile flattened out before settling back into place.

Brenna pulled at the sleeve of her gown. Surely the man could hear the sound of her heart pounding wildly in the cage of her chest, awaiting his answer? He glanced up to see Garrick staring at her, uncertainty flashing briefly before he sent her a lift of an eyebrow.

'Any news?' she asked.

'Nay. Sadly, he will not be able to join us for the wedding. His health is still poor, but he promises to host us for a visit after our trip.' He patted her arm and goose flesh rose along it.

That was not even close to what was written in that letter. She should know. She'd drafted the very words themselves, and Moira had written it out in as close to Father's hand as she could, using the letters they had brought with them for reference.

Brenna fidgeted with the end of her plait. 'That is disappointing,' she replied, trepidation filling her voice. It was not difficult to muster. Most likely she was standing next to a killer. Or perhaps merely one who ordered others to kill. Either way, she didn't wish to stay near him a moment longer, but if their plan was to work she had to play her part.

'Do not fret, my love. I have a wonderful surprise for you to distract you from such disappointing news.'

Brenna bet he did.

'Shall we sit?' Moira offered, gesturing them to follow on through the corridor.

They all went through the main hall with its large

banquet table into the sitting area, ladies first followed by the men. Garrick caught Rory's gaze and fisted his hands by his side. While Mr Winters was very English and bit too groomed for his liking, he did not seem the villain Garrick thought, or rather hoped, he might be, which made him even more dangerous. He was quite the wolf in sheep's clothing.

The tall, thin man with his dark pristine trousers, shockingly white tunic and vibrant maroon waist coat sat on the edge of the settee and ran a hand through his dark hair. He had a ring on his little finger with a family crest, and boots that reflected the sunlight. He looked exactly like what Garrick had expected: he looked like a bloody Englishman.

'Have you been able to make arrangements to bring Arthur and his son back to Oban, for their family's sake?' Brenna asked the moment they had all been seated. The dreaded Mr Winters placed a hand over hers and nodded.

'Of course, my darling. I've sent a man to see to it. Such a shame that you were attacked by thieves. Barbarians.'

'I don't believe the attack was random, but planned, and not by thieves. The men we encountered had training. They were quick, efficient and tracked incredibly well. They were also much better dressed than the average thief in these parts,' Garrick stated.

They also had your coin on their person.

He left that part out, eager to see what information he could gain without it. Playing the part of the serious soldier and protective suitor was quite easy. Too easy.

He reminded himself that Brenna was still to marry another, even if it would no longer be this scoundrel.

Mr Winters balked. 'Why would anyone be after Miss Stewart?'

'We believe they may have been after you, sir. You were supposed to be with Miss Stewart except you were called away at the last minute based on what Bren— Erm, Miss Stewart told us.'

A flicker of unease skittered across the man's brow before he rubbed his chin and answered. 'It was a last-minute decision. One that I regret now. To know that you were alone, left for dead. That you had to witness such an attack.'

'I am fortunate not to remember most of it,' Brenna murmured. 'And that Laird MacLean found me when he did.' She sent him a smile.

'Aye. It is quite the miracle,' Moira added.

'So, you do not believe that you could have been the target, sir?' Garrick slipped in another question.

He shrugged. 'I cannot imagine why. I don't have enemies and my business dealings are sound.'

Garrick sat back, knowing full well the man was now lying through his perfect white teeth. 'Anyone jealous of your pending marriage?'

Other than me.

He smiled. 'Most likely, but no one would harm her because of it.'

'It makes little sense. They came after her, then after us, to ensure she was dead. It seemed quite personal.' Garrick locked gazes with the man to see if he'd flinch.

'Like she was being hunted?' he asked, his gaze

zeroing in on Garrick. A flash of warning entered his eyes. His suppressed anger towards Garrick was unmistakable. Their ruse was working.

'Just like,' Garrick answered coolly, without missing a step in their verbal dance.

He dropped his gaze and gripped Brenna's hand. 'My dear, I—' His words broke off. 'I am so sorry. I don't understand how or why anyone would wish to harm you.' He tucked a lock of her hair behind her ear. She shifted on the settee, the colour draining from her face. He stilled, noting the change in her. 'We did have a break in the afternoon of your departure. They took the coin your father had brought along with some correspondence. Perhaps they believed you had more coin with you after they read the letters. Word of our pending nuptials is the talk of Oban.'

'Was anyone hurt?' Brenna asked, unable to hold her gaze.

'No. I was out handling business and the staff was out tending to duties to prepare for our nuptials.'

'I am glad to hear of it.' She met Garrick's gaze. 'Perhaps the answer is as simple as that. A robbery and then an attempt to steal more?'

'Perhaps.' His answer sounded as flat and dry as he'd hoped.

Garrick frowned. Mr Winters was a fine actor meant for the stage.

'Although your father is too ill to attend our wedding in Oban, perhaps your family and friends here could come? I would like you to all meet my family as well. They will love you all, of course.'

'There is no cause for the rush, Stephen. We could wait until Father is well enough to attend, or even marry in Glenhaven.' Brenna stated, shifting away from him.

Careful, Bren.

Winters noted the shift in her demeanour and moved closer to her, clasping her hand in his. 'I had hoped to surprise you, but a friend has helped me organise a journey for us to see all of Europe, but we must be on the boat by Thursday to depart on time. That is why I wished to hasten our union.'

Brenna gasped, her surprise genuine. 'Oh, my! That is…unexpected. I know not what to say.'

'Why? When we have children, we will not have such freedoms, but now is the perfect time for you to see the world with me.' He clutched her hands in his.

'I am merely surprised, that is all,' she replied.

'That is fine news,' Garrick added to try to help Brenna along.

Garrick mustered what strength he could and smiled at her. This was taking a toll on her, and now he had second thoughts. 'We would not miss attending your union for the world.'

'Then, it is settled. Brenna and I shall depart tonight, and you all shall join us in a few days' time to celebrate our nuptials. Perhaps we should not delay after all, but head back now. You look absolutely pale, my love.'

'She won't be travelling anywhere with you, Winters,' Garrick stated, rising from his chair and moving in closer to the man as he spoke.

He laughed. 'Why is that? We are engaged to be married, and I have come here to collect her by the laird's invitation. You have no stake in her future, Mac-Lean. I know full well you are laird of…nothing these days.' His eyes flashed a warning, a hint that the darkness in him would be bubbling to the surface soon.

'Because you are a cheat and a liar. What are you scheming at? We know you were involved in the attack on Brenna's carriage.' Garrick continued his approach and Rory began to move in to block Moira from the man's reach.

'And you are as daft as they come, MacLean.' Winters pulled a blade from his boot and had it at Brenna's throat before Garrick could reach him. 'I would hate to cut this pretty flesh,' he warned. 'Stay back. And order your men to clear a path, McKenna. I know you must have some ridiculous scheme to trap me, but she is my key to a safe passage.'

Brenna whimpered and leaned away from the blade, but Winters only increased his hold on her. It would take only a flick of the man's wrist to cut her throat.

Garrick's feet tingled and his ears buzzed. *Damn.* It couldn't happen again. *Not now. Not now.* He sucked in air through his mouth. His legs felt heavy, his body as if it belonged to someone else.

He couldn't fail her. Not now when she needed him most.

'While I do appreciate your offer of tea, Lady McKenna, I find I have worn out my welcome, so I'll be going…with my bride to be, of course. We have much to accomplish before we reach Oban.'

'I cannot say I will be sorry to see you leave, but you will unhand my sister,' Moira answered.

Rory edged closer and Winters tightened his hold, pricking Brenna's neck. A small thread of blood glided down her throat.

'Ah-ah, McKenna. One more step, and I might lose my grip.'

A tear slid down Brenna's cheek and Garrick held her gaze. 'Stay calm,' he told her. 'We will find you. You have my word.'

'Oh, I would not hold much promise in a rescue from him, my dear. He has had a rather poor record as of late. I believe your entire family is dead, isn't that right?' The man's dark eyes glistened in the light.

Everything around Garrick went silent. Rage coursed through his veins, and he commanded himself not to charge him. If he did, Brenna was as good as dead. 'You will die, Winters. That is a promise.'

The man laughed. 'Not by you,' he spat. 'Nor any of your men, McKenna. They had best provide me a clear path to my carriage where my driver awaits. I would hate my bride to have an accident before our nuptials.'

Chapter Twenty

Stephen shoved Brenna into the carriage, and she tumbled hard into the side of the squabs and onto the floor, scrambling up into the far corner of the seat in the darkness of the small space. The curtains were drawn and it had a remarkable likeness to a tomb: perhaps her own. She shivered and waited for her eyes to adjust to the darkness. If she could only find a weapon. If she could defend herself for a moment, she might be able to free herself and jump from the carriage. Heaven knew that whatever was outside would be better than being with him within. She hurriedly felt around the seat and the floor but found nothing.

Curses.

Winters entered, slammed the door shut and locked it before tapping his cane on the roof to signal for the carriage to be off. The carriage lurched off with a sudden start, sending her backwards into the seat, and her head hit the back of it.

'Careful, pet,' Winters snarled.

'As if you care,' she snapped.

She watched him. Perhaps if she challenged him, he would make a mistake and she could free herself. 'It must be quite tiring to hide your madness. You genuinely had me fooled. I just believed you to be an arrogant dullard.'

'Are you trying to make me kill you?' he asked, peeling the gloves from his hands. 'It will not work. Too much is at stake.'

She frowned. Another tactic would be necessary, but what?

'How is your father?' he asked.

She narrowed her eyes at him, unsure of his change in topic. 'The same. He is ailing, as you well know.'

'Near death, I do hope,' he answered. His cold, dark eyes met her own.

She gasped. 'What have you done?'

'Nothing yet, but I have men in place in case they are needed. My hope is that your death will cause him to succumb to his illness. The death of a youngest child, a daughter as pretty as you, will come at some cost. But, if not, there are other means.'

'Sorry to disappoint, but I do not plan to die any time soon.' She gripped the bottom of her carriage seat.

'We shall see. This whole business is very tiresome, but it will be over soon. By my estimates, I will be settled at home this eve free of a future wife and father-in-law, but full of the coin from your coffers and those from the King for having set such chaos in motion.' He set his full gaze upon her and the cruelty within its depths chilled her. 'All part of a greater plan. One far more important than just you and I. Your sacrifice is needed for England's future.'

'Sacrifice?' Her stomach pitted.

'Yes. When we met your father and realised his level of desperation to secure more power and safety for the future of the Stewarts, your clan was the perfect mark. Enlist the laird's help in helping to ease tensions between England and Scotland, while promising him protection as well as a gainful marriage for his daughter. And the sot asked few questions. I can only assume it was because he cared little about the truth. He just needed you settled before he died.' He smiled at her. 'And you will be. Just a bit further under the ground than you may have planned.'

'It is too late for you, Winters. We knew of your plan and have already sent word to my family, as well as the Camerons. Everyone will already know of your scheme. Marrying me will secure you nothing.'

He studied her and tilted his head. 'Hmm. Well, I had planned for the interference from McKenna and your own family, but I did forget that blasted alliance your brother-in-law has with the Camerons.' He smiled. 'But I am sure I can concoct a way to shift the blame to them. From what I hear, the Camerons have many enemies, as they are so large and powerful. Perhaps I can pool the other clans against them.' He nodded. 'Yes, yes, I shall do that. It may delay things a day or two, but in the end it will make the chaos in the Highlands even more extensive.'

She gaped at him. 'You truly are mad. You cannot merely turn clans against one another on a whim. It is not a chess game. Thousands of lives are at stake.' She leaned forward in her seat.

He pulled an extravagant pocket watch from his coat pocket and opened it. 'Your family at Blackmore should be dispatched within the next hour or two by my men. And, now that I think upon it, I am rather sure our vicar can produce a marriage licence with or without your blessing.'

He returned it to his pocket and pulled a small roped cord out in its place. 'So, I best be on with it. You must all be dead by nightfall for my plan to stay on its new course.'

He frowned, winding the rope around one of his hands. 'Although, it is a pity. You are quite pretty in your own way, even if you won't stop yapping about.' He lunged forward with the rope.

Brenna scrabbled away from him to the other end of the bench seat, her limbs flailing against him. Her mind whirled as she kicked and screamed to free herself from him. She had to save herself so she could warn her family at Blackmore and Glenhaven to protect them from whatever horrors Winters and his men had sent their way, but how? She landed a blow to his shin, and he cursed. She prayed it wasn't already too late.

As soon as Winters' carriage roared out of the drive, Rory shouted orders to his most trusted and valued manservant, Angus. 'Add more men to the watch, alert the Camerons and lock down Blackmore. No one goes in and out except for me and Laird MacLean.'

'Aye, my laird,' Angus answered and disappeared down the front steps.

'And I will go after Brenna,' Garrick stated. 'If I hurry, I may be able to catch up with her carriage before it is too late.' His gut tightened and every fibre of his body seized in agony over the idea that he might be. All because he had frozen up. Again.

'You will, my friend. You will.'

Garrick prayed to God that his friend was right.

He jogged to the barn, saddled up Montgomerie and rode him at neck-breaking speed out of the slick grounds of Blackmore and along the road that paralleled the cliffs overlooking the Firth of Lorn. As the only road wide enough to allow for a carriage, it would have been the only route possible for Winters and Brenna to have taken. Now it was only a matter of whether he could intercept them soon enough.

Dirt and snow kicked up behind him as he rode low against Montgomerie's lean form. After several minutes, Garrick saw the carriage, sunset glistening off the black lacquer sheen as it roared far too quickly down the road. The man was not only mad but reckless. At any moment, one of the horses could lose their footing or a wheel hit a rut, sending the carriage out of control. Regardless of the danger, relief sang through Garrick's body at the knowledge that he could save her. He eased up on Montgomerie's reins to steady his approach along the narrowing pass. Just then, the carriage jerked wildly to the left and then the right, skittering dangerously close to the cliff's edge and the water below.

'Stop!' Garrick called to the driver.

The man turned, saw him and clapped the reins along the horses' sides to drive them on faster.

Saints be. The fool of a man would get them all killed. He sped up and travelled along a parallel track above them, as he'd run out of space along the road to ride alongside. His idea was foolish and reckless, perhaps even more so than the driver's. He hesitated. The side door of the carriage flew open and Brenna screamed as she slid partly out of the moving carriage. Her arms clung to the small handle and she pulled herself back in. The door swung back open and clapped along the side of the carriage as it continued on.

Garrick's heart dropped. His legs tingled. He had to jump now, no matter what happened. Brenna was running out of time and soon he would be at the edge of his own path and unable to follow any longer. He had to jump and stop that carriage. He yanked Montgomerie to a halt, dismounted, ran along the hillside until there was no more earth beneath him and leapt with all his might.

Brenna screamed as her upper body felt the rush of cold air around her and saw the drop to the loch below.

Stephen laughed, before yanking her back inside the carriage. The door clapped against the side as they barrelled down the slushy road, the wheels spraying up wet snow as they went.

'Sir?' the driver called down to him, swerving again. 'Shall I stop?'

'Keep on, Edward!' Stephen growled. 'Go faster.

My fiancée and I are coming to an agreement about the role she shall play in my life. Give us but a moment to sort it out.'

He shoved her out again, for longer this time, before yanking her back in.

Brenna paled as she clutched his forearm. She panted for breath and shivered at the knowledge she was going to die at the hands of a madman.

'What shall you do now?' He snickered.

When she didn't answer, he shrugged. 'Just as I told my mother before you left. You are nothing. A vapid space covered in beauty. Other than a good poke, you are useless. Bloody useless.'

Useless?

Rage erupted from her and she lifted her hand to slap him, digging her nails into his fine pasty cheek. 'I am not useless!'

'You bitch!' he exclaimed, clutching her neck by the throat. 'Beauty can be so easily replaced. I hope you can swim. If you survive the drop, that is. It matters not to me.'

He grinned and she gasped for air, clawing at his hand and wrist to release its hold on her neck. He growled as she dug her nails into his flesh, drawing blood along his hand.

He cursed again and squeezed harder.

'Stop! Stop the carriage!' a voice boomed from above them.

Garrick. Thank God.

Distracted, Stephen loosened his hold momentarily, and Brenna freed herself. She sucked in greedy breaths and coughed as she struggled to get air back into her lungs and scoot away from him.

'Sir?' the driver called back. 'Shall I stop?'

'Nay, fool. Go faster,' Stephen shouted.

He returned his wrath to Brenna, sliding over to her as the carriage jostled them around as it picked up speed. 'You must be dead for me to fulfil my orders to the King. The Stewarts must be ended one by one, and the clan erased from the Highlands.'

'Erased?' She coughed, clutching her throat and watching his approach. 'You cannot erase thousands of people. You are mad.'

'Perhaps I am mad, but it can be done. Isn't that what happened to your Laird MacLean?' He snickered again. 'Some of my finest work, my dear.'

Her blood chilled. 'You did that?' she asked. How could one man end a people?

'Yes. How else was I to bring down your own clan? We could not have you two marrying. That would have only strengthened the Highlands.'

'You will pay for what you have done,' Brenna promised. And he would. She just needed to survive this first.

A thud sounded atop the carriage, and it lurched hard to the right towards the cliffs, sending them both sliding towards the open carriage door, which still clapped against the sides as they raced down the hill. She glanced out, saw the loch far below and regretted it. A wave of dizziness washed over her. Why couldn't they have been driving on a flat stretch of road by a stream instead? She cringed.

He lunged for her, and she slid deftly out of his reach as the carriage pitched to the side again. 'You were never quite so urgent for my attentions when we met,' she chided, trying to focus on something other than the perilous drop below if she got much closer to the open door.

'I'm quite eager to be rid of you before we run out of cliff, so I can enjoy the money from your father and the King. I also do not like being a fiancé. I prefer my freedom.' He held onto the handle of the other, still-closed carriage door and stretched out as far as he could. He grabbed for her. Unable to move any further away without falling out of the open door, she was caught in the vice of his hold on her forearm. He wrenched her arm and she cried out as her arm burned from the force of his hold. If she could hang on a bit longer, they'd be out of danger, as the turn in road away from the cliffs was just ahead.

'Hang on, Bren! Slow the carriage!' Garrick shouted from the bench seat.

The driver cried out and then flew from the bench seat of the moving carriage onto the road to their left. He crashed to the ground.

'Looks like you will be in need of a new driver,' she murmured.

'He is as replaceable as you are,' Winters sneered, yanking her away from the seat and closer to the open door.

She screamed, scrambling for a hold on the door, but lost her grip. She pitched to the side and clawed into his arm for purchase. He attempted to kick her away, but the carriage swerved as Garrick pulled the horses' reins to slow them, sending Stephen in the opposite direction towards her and the door that clapped precariously against the side of the carriage.

She wrapped one arm around the seat to hold herself as Stephen slid past her and partially out of the open door. He clung to her arm. Her eyes watered at the strain of his weight pulling against her shoulder and her grip on the seat.

'Pull me up,' he commanded as his torso dragged along the cliffside and he attempted to get his footing as the carriage slowed.

She cried out in agony as her fingers slid from the seat. Stephen's weight was too much for her to counter. As they bumped along, his hold on her arm loosened.

Just hold on a minute longer.

He yanked on her arm. 'If I go, you go!' He laughed.

She cried out as her fingers lost their hold on the seat and she fell through the open carriage door.

She hit the ground hard, even though the carriage wasn't moving as fast as it had been, and felt the air along her legs as her body pitched over the side of the cliff. Stephen's hand slid off her forearm and she heard his yell as he cascaded down into the waters below. Her flailing hands closed around the flat edge of a boulder as her legs swung in the air. She sighed in relief.

She wasn't dead. Yet.

The waters of the loch crashed against the shoreline below as she stared up at the sky. She screamed, but it sounded hollow and empty. Had Garrick even heard her? How long could she hold on?

Carefully, she pulled herself up slowly until she was hugging the boulder to her chest, her arms shaking from the effort to hold on. Her teeth chattered from the wind and cold.

'Bren? Bren?' Garrick called from above.

'I am here,' she cried out.

He ran to her and skidded to the ground, extending his arm over the side. He couldn't quite reach her. Her stomach bottomed out.

He met her gaze. 'Take my hand,' he said.

What?

She shook her head, her body vibrating from fear. She'd been too high for too long. 'I can't... I can't let go.'

'You have to. Trust me.'

She shook her head. 'I'm slipping. If I let go, I'll drop into the loch.'

Thinking of the loch, how far up she was and how far it was below made her dizzy, and she squeezed her eyes shut.

'Bren,' Garrick murmured, his tone softened. 'Trust me.'

The insides of her floated, light as air. Did she dare? Would she fall if she did? She knew she would die if she didn't. She opened her eyes and met his gaze, his green eyes steady and certain, and nodded.

Then, with one big breath, she let go of her right hand and reached up while still holding on with her left, and as soon as she did he grabbed her by the arm. Instead of plummeting to her death, she was pulled up until she was close enough for him to reach her with both arms.

When she was entirely on the ground, she flopped back, eager to feel the weight of firm land and solid earth beneath her torso.

Garrick leaned over her, his eyes bright, his breath coming out in uneven pants. He brushed back the hair from her face and cupped her cheek with his palm. The warm, strong feel of him made her eyes close in relief. 'Are you hurt?'

'Nay,' she panted, covering his hand with her own, letting her heart slow as she settled into the knowledge that he was there, and they were safe. 'But you must get us back to Blackmore. Mr Winters has much more ruin planned.'

'I will. Catch your breath first. You almost died.' The husky hitch in his voice made her open her eyes. The pad of his thumb rubbed gently on her cheek.

'Thank you,' she whispered, reaching up to him.

'For what?' he asked, leaning into her touch as her fingertips skimmed his neck.

'For saving me...again.'

He pulled her into an embrace, hugging her fiercely, whispering into her hair. 'Always, Bren. I will always move heaven and earth for you.'

As she clutched him to her, she wished he could be hers, that he could let the past go, but she knew deep in her soul that he still held his pain and shame as close to his heart as he held her to him now.

Chapter Twenty-One

'It is a miracle you are both alive,' Moira said. She'd fussed over Brenna and Garrick since they had returned to Blackmore. Each had been tucked in tartans, given copious amounts of tea and sat huddled on the settees in front of the burning hearth in the main hall. Brenna feared her sister might dissolve with worry.

'Moira, please sit down and rest.' Brenna reached for her sister's hand as she walked by her.

'How can I possibly sit?' She paced in front of the hearth. 'You were almost killed, we have no idea if Ewan and Father are well and who knows how many more of these men are set on destroying us? Sit? Ridiculous.' She shook her head.

Rory walked up behind her and wrapped his arms around her waist. 'No one is being ridiculous. There is nothing we can do as of this very moment. We have sent word to everyone we can, and have added extra soldiers to guard Blackmore, as well as the border between us and the Camerons. They also are on high alert.

If there is anyone in this scheme left to be found, we will find them.'

'I find your certainty appalling,' Moira answered, her lip quirking up.

'As do I,' Garrick agreed.

Fatigue pressed in on Brenna. Now that the rush of energy and fear of almost being killed and needing to get word to Glenhaven about what they'd learned from Stephen had run its course, it felt as if her bones had turned to oats. She yawned into her hand.

Escaping death was tiresome.

'Tomorrow I will leave for Glenhaven,' Garrick announced.

Brenna blinked and sat up. 'Why?'

'To ensure your family is well.'

She shook her head. 'Garrick, there is a strong possibility you would be killed along your journey. Stephen alluded to this being a large-scale scheme with who knows how many men involved. Men may be looking for you even now. And you have not even healed from your initial injuries from before. Rescuing me has ripped out your stitches. You are oozing blood even now.' She gestured to his wound.

'Would you prefer I stand by and do nothing?'

She quirked her lips. 'You have not exactly been standing by and doing nothing.'

'Perhaps not, but I have failed you in letting you almost marry that man, and my own clan and family by not being there to protect them. But I can help your family now. You must let me.' The desperation in his green eyes and the strained pitch of his voice stilled her.

The agony he felt matched her own. She had also been part of this horrid scheme. She had agreed to marry a man she did not know to please her father, even though she didn't wish to, and she'd never asked for details.

It was high time she also gained her footing in this world and sought her own place in it with purpose. And speaking with Father was the first step in doing that.

'We go together.'

'What? You just proclaimed it was not safe.' He frowned at her.

'It isn't, but I need to return home. And there is no one else I trust more with my safety…than you.'

The air between them stilled and his eyes softened, the longing in them telling her all she needed to know. He loved her as she did him, despite all they'd endured. But she also knew that too much needed to be settled to reclaim any of that love or passion between them just yet. And, without that, they'd never survive the future, no matter how much they cared for one another. Love could not exist in a space without trust and one full of fear. Letting go of the past would take work from both of them, but she knew she was willing to do it. She just needed to see if he was.

'Aye,' he answered. 'Then, we will go together.'

'Now I shall never be able to sit again,' Moira quipped.

'Well, then, we shall just stand together until they return,' Rory teased.

Angus hurried into the hall. 'Sir, y'er needed.'

'What is it?' Rory asked, his body stiffening in alarm.

'A man's been found at the edge of the grounds. Sean found him.'

'Take us to him.' Rory commanded. He fell into step with Angus, and Garrick wasn't far behind.

As they reached the barn, Sean waved to them from far off in the meadow. He stood at the break between meadows and deep forest. They jogged to him and, once they arrived, Garrick's stomach dropped.

'This is the other man who was in the party searching for us when we fled Loch Linnhe.'

'Are you sure?' Rory asked.

'The scars on his face are unmistakable. It is him.'

'Why would he be dead here?' Rory asked.

'Have you searched him?' Garrick stooped to get a closer look at the man who appeared to have been felled by a large blade to the gut.

Sean shook his head, his face pale.

Garrick searched the man's coat pockets and found nothing. He then searched the man's trews to see if he'd hidden anything further on his person. He pulled two letters from him. He cursed.

'One of these is addressed to you, Rory.' The other had no identifying information on the outside of it.

Rory took the letter addressed to him and opened it. 'This was the letter from the Camerons that we had been expecting. They have nothing good to report on Winters.'

'Evidently Winters knew that and intercepted the letter somehow.'

'How would they even know we sent such an enquiry?'

'Perhaps he has allies, as we do, and used them to prevent this information from getting to Brenna in time.'

'And it might have worked, had you not intercepted the other letters, and we received word from Uncle's other contacts in Oban regarding some of his questionable business dealings.' Rory rested his hands on his waist.

Garrick opened the other letter and scanned it. 'This is a map.'

Rory read over his shoulder. 'Of the Highlands.'

'Aye.' His heart raced and then dropped into his stomach, stealing his breath. There in bold lettering was a map of all the clan borders in the Highlands. Of great interest were the four to the north of Blackmore: MacLean, Stewart, Cameron, MacDougall. MacLean and MacDougall had an X through them.

'They are destroying us one by one, just as Brenna said Winters was boasting of. And, by the looks of this, the Stewarts are definitely next.'

'We cannot wait until the morrow. I must go at once before it is too late.' Garrick sprinted out to the barn. Rory ran alongside him.

'They cannot destroy Bran and the Stewarts,' Rory challenged as they reached Montgomerie's stall.

'And I did not think they could bring down the MacDougalls, or my own people either. But our clans and lands have been splintered and scattered in a handful of months. By continuing to destroy us one by one, the

King will get his wish of a complete elimination of our people, won't he?'

Rory balked. He shook his head. 'I cannot fathom it.'

'This union with the Stewarts was no union but a means of bringing down the entire clan.'

Rory gripped Garrick's shoulder. 'All the more reason for you to have a plan before you ride off into the night. We will meet with my men, send out new missives by messengers to ensure their safety before your arrival and you and Brenna will rest before you collapse where you stand.'

'I hate it when you are right.' Garrick frowned.

Rory smirked. 'I know.'

The return journey to Glenhaven was an uneventful and quick one, as they had a carriage and fresh horses changed out along the way, so they did not have to pause along their journey. They slept soundly in the carriage, with soldiers riding alongside them as they went, and the days it would have taken due to the snow hampering their journey were reduced. They arrived at Glenhaven two days later without incident.

As the carriage rolled to a stop, Garrick's chest tightened. Although all seemed as it should, with soldiers posted outside the castle walls and main doors, he wouldn't feel any relief until the soldiers that rode alongside them checked the area and returned with a report that all was indeed well at Glenhaven.

'I do not know what I shall do if anything has happened to them,' Brenna whispered. She studied the castle doors.

He took her chilled hand in his and squeezed it briefly before letting go. 'Whatever has come to pass, we will face it together.'

'Aye.'

The castle doors opened and Ewan Stewart, Brenna's older brother, emerged.

'Ewan!' Brenna's hand flew to her mouth and her eyes filled with tears. The soldier waved to them that all was secure, and Brenna rushed from the carriage and into her brother's arms.

Garrick watched from a distance, not wishing to crowd their moment. A deep ache filled his chest. He would never have such a moment with his siblings again, and the agony of it seized him anew. He swallowed the emotion. Knowing he could give this to Brenna lightened some of his loss, so he clung to her joy as if it were his own.

When she turned to him and waved for him to come in, he smiled, eased from the carriage and remembered this could still be his, but he had to choose it. And, in order to choose it freely, he had to be whole again and the man he used to be. Taking a deep breath, he approached. Each step towards her was a step away from the safe, dark place of isolation and shame and into the light of uncertainty tinged with hope.

'Ewan.' He nodded to Brenna's brother as he approached. He'd aged since he'd last seen him, and an edge of wariness pulled down the corners of his eyes.

'Garrick.' He clapped him on the shoulder. 'Thank you for all you have done for Brenna and for us. We owe you a great debt. We have secured Glenhaven and sent word to our people. We are on watch for any further threats from Winters and his men because of your warning. I believe many lives have been spared.'

Garrick nodded, feeling awkward and uncertain under such praise.

'I am glad all is well. I was fearful the warnings would not reach you in time. How is Father?' Brenna asked as they followed Ewan inside.

'He will be better knowing you are both here, alive and well.'

Garrick did not miss the forced pitch in the man's voice. Brenna's smile fell. Evidently, she noticed it as well.

'May I see him now?'

'Of course. I will take you to him.'

Garrick's steps faltered. 'I will allow you some privacy,' he offered.

Ewan turned. 'He wishes to see you too, Garrick. Join us.'

Garrick hesitated. Did he wish to see Bran? The man who had believed him dead and almost married off his daughter to a murderer, all to gain favour with the King? Not really. But, when Brenna's expectant gaze met his, he nodded. 'Certainly.'

As they entered Bran Stewart's chamber, the smell of sickness and the horrid stench of ointments and other cures assailed Garrick. He sucked in a breath to steady himself. He was shocked to see that the once strong, dominant man full of bluster was now a small, diminished figure propped up in his bed on a sea of pillows, his features sunken and flat. At the sight of Brenna, light came back into the man's eyes, and he struggled to straighten up.

Garrick's heart squeezed for Brenna as she forced a smile and rushed to his bedside.

Thank God they'd come when they had. It did not take a doctor to know this man had not long left in this world. It pained him to know Moira had not come as well.

'Daughter.' Bran spoke and hugged her to him. 'The sight of you warms me.' She pressed a kiss to his cheek.

'Garrick,' he called, reaching out a shaky hand to him.

Steady.

He came to the other side of his bed, and the sight of him so ill cut Garrick to the bone. Red puffy eyes rested amongst the shadows beneath and pale pallor of his face. Had he lost so much weight since he'd last seen him? Garrick's stomach curdled as he took the man's once fierce grip into his own, hardly feeling the pressure of his hold on his flesh as he greeted him.

He set his warrior mask in place, so Brenna would not read the emotion gurgling beneath. He needed to be strong for her, and he would be.

'I am for ever in your debt for rescuing Brenna, not once but twice.' His gaze dropped. 'Especially when I am to blame.'

The man's words shook him. Had Bran just acknowledged a failing? Garrick glanced at Ewan, who nodded to him. This must be the new Bran, the one attempting to right his wrongs before it was too late, and Garrick would not deny him that, no matter the past. No matter what he had said and done to his daughter and the slight he had given Garrick by refusing him as son-in-law.

'No one could have known the plan they had in place, Bran. We were lucky to have had such great support from the Camerons and the McKennas. Without them, we would not be here.'

He nodded. 'Please give them my thanks.'

Brenna's lip quivered. 'You will get well and tell them yourself, Father. You cannot just give up. The physicians said you could improve.'

'I will leave you two to speak,' Garrick offered, knowing he needed to give Brenna this time with him.

'Thank you, my son. Thank you for what you have done for both of my daughters.'

Garrick pressed a hand to the man's shoulder. 'I will always protect them. You have my word.'

'If you need me, Bren, I'll just be outside the chamber door.'

'And I've work to attend to Father. I will leave you.' Ewan stepped out of the room.

Brenna kissed her brother's cheek and then met Garrick's gaze, her eyes bright blue pools of sorrow, and he couldn't breathe. As she nodded to him, a tear slid down her cheek.

Chapter Twenty-Two

Bran Stewart was a shell of the domineering, controlling man he'd always been. As Brenna stared at him, she wondered what she had ever been afraid of. Her father was like everyone else: he was human, he had frailties and he was not guaranteed to live for ever.

But he'd also lied to her, manipulated her and almost got her killed. And, sick or not, he would answer for those decisions. She needed to know before he died why he had been so cruel and why she could never earn his praise and affections.

She wiped her eyes, pulled back her shoulders and said what she'd rehearsed in her head over the last two days before she lost her nerve. 'Why did you lie to me, Father? You made me believe I was choosing to marry Mr Winters to please you and gain your favour, but you had already promised me to him. It was no choice at all.'

'Daughter,' he said, the gruff tightness she was long used to back in his voice. 'You cannot understand the duties and responsibilities of a laird. But Ewan will soon.'

'That is exactly what I mean,' Brenna answered, frustration boiling beneath her skin. 'I almost died trying to earn your favour and yet you still will not tell me the truth because I am not Ewan or Moira. I can understand your responsibilities, Father. I am not obtuse or addled.'

'You will not speak to me as such!' he boomed.

'It is time I did,' she countered. 'I deserve your respect and truth.'

He stared at her. 'Do you?'

She shivered and her voice quavered. 'I do,' she replied, crossing her arms against her chest. 'And I do not understand why you have always viewed me as less than I am. I am more than a mere decoration in this household.'

She faltered after the words had escaped her lips. They had always ignored their issues and failings. Speaking of them seemed unnatural and awkward, and somehow a betrayal to him. Even with all of his unkind words and horrid decisions, he was still her father, and he always would be. What if these were the last words they shared with one another? Her throat dried. But at least she would have asked. She would have tried to understand. She would have finally stood up for herself.

He stared off, anger furrowing his brow.

She tried once more. 'Tell me why you see me as so useless to you, Father. I deserve to know that, after all that has happened. Do not deny me the truth.'

He shifted on his bed. 'Why can you not let it be?'

'Leaving things *be* almost killed me. You and I both know you are sick. We may not get another chance. Why can you not just be honest with me?'

He cursed under his breath and sighed, pressing deeper into the folds of the pillows. He looked heavenward. 'I never tried with you as I did with Moira and Ewan. You reminded me too much of your mother.'

Her eyes filled with emotion. 'Did I?'

'Aye. After she died, I could scarce stand to be in the room with you, you reminded me of her so, and my grief consumed me. The older you became, the more you were a mirror of her. Under all of the trappings of fashion and gowns and beauty, you had a kindness and light that others responded to just like she did. *You* bring people back together, add peace to a person's heart just by looking at them. You held us together, our little family, after your mother passed, didn't you? Always in the thick of it with your brother and sister, and fussing over me and keeping me well, even when I was not grateful and batted you away like a fly. And the things I have said to you over the years, lass…'

Were those tears she saw in his eyes?

'Come here,' he commanded.

She hesitated but approached him and walked into his embrace. He hugged her close to him and kissed her head. 'I am sorry, so sorry. They were the opposite of the truth. And I want you to live the rest of your days knowing that. Promise me you'll remember this and not the past.'

'Aye. I will.'

'Good. That is all I ask.'

She turned and met his gaze. 'Is it?'

'For now.' He winked at her.

'Now, that is the father I know.' She sniffed and wiped her eyes, grateful to be set free by knowing the truth behind his cruelties at last.

The squeak of Bran's chamber door opened, giving Garrick a start. It was merely a maid bringing in fresh linens and a basin of water. He glanced at the clock. It was midday, and he would need to leave soon to reach Westmoreland by nightfall. Of course, he hadn't told Brenna of his plan, and now that he'd seen the state of Bran he was reluctant to leave her.

He also knew he was desperately trying to find reasons to avoid the truth that such a journey would bring and the agony an acknowledgment of what he had lost would cost him.

Ewan approached. 'Brenna still in there?'

'Aye.'

Ewan sat down on the bench next to him outside the chamber door. 'I stepped out a while ago to give them some privacy. I have an update on Winters and his scheme.'

'Oh?' Garrick lifted his brow. 'What have you learned?'

'Word of the man's planned destruction of the clans has been relayed to all of the lairds and chiefs and spread like wildfire through the villages. As we speak, the traitors are being rooted out one by one. We are united even more tightly now that the threat from the King and his men has been brought to light. I believe in time the Highlands will be safer and stronger than ever.' Ewan smiled.

'That is an unexpected miracle.'

'My thoughts exactly. You and Brenna may have saved us all.'

Garrick nodded at the irony. *If only we could save each other and our future together.* But he didn't know how to do that. Not yet, anyway.

'How are you?' Ewan asked.

How did one begin to answer such a question?

'Alive.'

Ewan leaned forward, resting his elbows on his knees. 'Sorry for the believing you were dead part. I should have known better.' He smiled up at Garrick.

'Aye. Seems I'm indestructible in most ways. Even if I don't wish to be.'

Ewan shook his head. 'Give yourself some time. It has to be quite a shock to return with everything so... changed.'

'That's a polite way to put it.'

Ewan shook his head. 'If we had known what was happening, we would have interceded. It was a horrid to know what had been done. It sent Father reeling. All he could think of was preventing that from...' He paused as he caught what he was about to say.

'Happening to you? From being as unlucky as us?' Garrick tilted his head. 'Who could blame him?'

'There wasn't much we could do afterwards, but we gathered volunteers to go with us to Westmoreland and the surrounding lands to bury the dead.'

Garrick gripped the seat of the bench, steeling himself from the raw emotion tightening his chest. 'That is a great kindness to me and my people. Thank you.'

Ewan hesitated, his Adam's apple bobbing in his throat. 'I know you would have done the same for us without question.'

He nodded. He would have.

'Your mother and brother were brought to the family plot. We placed them next to your father and brother.'

He nodded, blinking rapidly to keep the flood of emotion at bay. 'Aye. That is where they would have wanted to be.'

What was he doing here? Why wasn't he there already? Putting off the past wouldn't change it.

He bolted up, unable to sit a moment longer. 'May I borrow a horse?'

'Of course.'

'Tell Brenna I left for Westmoreland and will return on the morrow. There is something that I cannot put off a moment longer.'

'Garrick…' Ewan called after him. 'I am sorry. Sorry beyond words.'

As am I. As am I.

Once the cool fresh air of the outdoors hit his face, Garrick sighed. Soon, the tingling in his limbs subsided. He couldn't stay inside the castle a moment longer. The tide of sorrow had pressed in on him heavy and thick, and he couldn't breathe. Once his heart stopped hammering in his ears, he headed to the stables. While he couldn't take Montgomerie after such a long ride the last few days to reach Glenhaven, he would borrow a stallion and head to Westmoreland.

He could set aside his grief and duty no longer. Even if he was a laird of nothing and no one, he still held the title of Laird Garrick MacLean of Westmoreland. He would see to the end of it, no matter how broken it made him. If he truly wanted to attempt a new beginning with Brenna, he had to face the past and his part in it, wherever it might lead. It was the only way to know if they had a whisper of a chance of a future.

He mounted his borrowed steed and headed out without looking back. Soon the distance melted away and he brought his horse to a halt, as he had but a week prior at the base of the hillside, looking up at the haunting profile of Westmoreland in the moonlight. He'd half hoped to see the MacLean crest whipping in the wind at the highest turret, but it wasn't there among the dusky night sky. He frowned. In fact, no flag flew in the air, and no torches glowed in the distance within or about the castle save one small flickering light in the old grounds keep, due east of the castle.

He was in no mood for surprises, and without reinforcements, but he couldn't turn back or he'd never return. He wasn't strong enough to make this journey a third time, knowing what he did about what he would discover upon his arrival. He was too broken.

He rode in as far as he dared before dismounting and walking the rest of the way to the keep. While Westmoreland was supposed to have been captured and taken over by an English duke for a residence, it seemed unoccupied. Overgrowth that had since died back in the cold clogged the paths, and the drive was not smooth but scarred with pits and holes that could injure a horse or break a carriage wheel. No duke would be living here. Not like this. A branch snapped ahead outside the small keep, and Garrick silently drew his blade from his waist belt.

While he didn't wish to battle anyone, if he had to down a man to get to the truth of what had happened to his home and his family and find peace, he would. The smell of wood smoke and stew filled the air and Garrick's stomach rumbled. He grimaced. Perfect timing. He hadn't eaten since he'd broken his fast that morn, and his body reminded him of his poor choice at the most inopportune time.

Taking one step and then another, he silently reached the window of the keep. A fire burned in the hearth and a small pot bubbled over the fire. The keep was cosy and tended to. *Occupied.* Someone was living there and had been for some time. Had the duke left the castle in the care of a single man? None of it made any sense.

'Dinn'a take another step,' a man warned.

Garrick froze. 'And if I do?' he challenged.

'My laird?' The old man stepped into the light.

'Phineas!' Garrick rushed to the man and pulled him into an embrace.

'I knew ye would return,' the old man said. 'Let me look at ye.' Phineas wiped a tear from his eye as he pulled back to take the sight of Garrick in.

'It does me well to see you,' Garrick said. 'I thought to never see any MacLeans again.' He pressed his hand to his chest where his heart soared with hope. The old man had been the groundskeeper for as long as Garrick could remember. His long, wavy grey hair was even whiter than he remembered, but his pale blue eyes were the same. Soft, kind and full of wisdom.

'Come, come.' He waved Garrick in. 'I've just started some stew. Join me.'

'I would love to,' Garrick answered and followed him into the keep. The small space was neat, tidy and cared for, unlike the rest of Westmoreland. The Mac-Lean tartan draped over the end of the man's meagre bed made Garrick's heart soar with pride.

The clan was not erased yet. A few of them remained.

'So, where have ye been?' the man asked, stirring the stew as he stood over the fire.

'Not here, unfortunately.'

'And Ayleen?' he asked.

'Nay. She is gone. I could not save her.' The truth made his mouth ache. Somehow telling him seemed easier than saying it to himself.

'Ack.' He shook his head. 'I am sorry to hear. Sweet lass she was.'

He nodded. 'Aye. A great loss…to everyone.'

'The MacLeans have had many losses as of late. I assume ye come from hearing the news of what has come to pass?'

Heat flushed his body and he shifted on his feet. 'Aye.'

Phineas stood and went to a small table with two chairs. 'Sit. It needs to simmer. I've something for ye.'

Garrick settled into one of the two chairs and rested his hands on the table. He slid his fingertips over the rippled grain in the wood, the slight friction soothing as he awaited the man's return. Phineas sat opposite him and placed a small wooden box on the table.

The sight of it made his eyes well. His mother's jewellery box. He blinked back the emotion, but it thrust forward, and he wiped a tear from his eye.

'She never believed ye had died. Said she would have known. Would have felt the sorrow in her bones. Asked me to save it for ye for when ye returned.'

Garrick wiped a hand over his mouth and then reached over to open the lid. His mother's wedding ring and locket lay next to the laird's ring with the MacLean family crest on it. Garrick had left it for Cairn to wear in his absence. His baby brother had been so proud to be acting laird. His eyes welled as his thumb skimmed the cool silver surface. He'd been far too young to die. And far too good. Unlike him.

'He wanted ye to wear it again,' Phineas added. 'Said ye were too bloody stubborn to die.'

Garrick laughed, choking on the sob of grief sitting in the back of his throat. 'I think God was just too busy to get to me.'

'Nay,' Phineas answered, his blue eyes meeting his gaze. ''Tis not yer time.'

Garrick wasn't so sure.

'The duke up and abandoned the place after a few months. Too isolated, and the wife didn'a like it. Too cold and lonely.' He rolled his eyes. 'Feckless the lot of them. Glad to see them leave. Wish I could have driven them out meself, but I am not the young man I once was.'

'As do I.'

A letter with his name on it rested beneath the jewellery and, although Garrick wanted to read it, he didn't know if he dared. Was he ready? He closed the lid. He wasn't.

Phineas nodded. 'Should be ready. Hungry?'

'Aye,' Garrick replied, wiping his eyes. Some food would definitely help. He knew he had to face the past, but he didn't have to do it all at once or on an empty stomach.

Phineas filled two bowls, returned with spoons and then brought them each a tankard of ale.

'Is it just you out here? Alone?' Garrick blew on the hot stew even though he longed to devour it.

'Aye. I stayed on when the duke came. I wanted to be here when you returned. I promised your mother. I kept my word.'

The first spoonful went down hard on the knowing that Phineas had stayed because of him and out of devotion to his family. Phineas was a far better man than Garrick could ever be, and yet here he was in this tiny keep.

'Everyone else?' he dared ask.

'Many were lost in the uprising. They tried to stop what was happening. Protect your mother and Cairn. Protect Westmoreland and the lands. But the more we resisted, the more brutal the retaliation from the King's men became. In the end, Cairn commanded them to cease their fighting and leave, so they scattered to other parts of the Highlands and were accepted into other clans. His command saved us in the end.'

'Cairn,' Garrick muttered, clenching his jaw.

Phineas smiled. 'Ye would have been proud of him. Brave. Acted like the man ye knew he could be when ye left him in charge.'

'I am proud, so proud.' Nausea made his stomach clench around the little food he had eaten. 'But I am also sick with grief.' He pounded the table with his fist and the bowls and spoons clattered from the force. 'I killed them by not being here. I did that. I killed them all.' The dam of emotion burst within him, and Garrick sobbed, so loudly and for so long that he did not know if it would ever cease.

The old man reached over and gripped his forearm when the torrent of emotion finally subsided. 'Nay, son. Ye did not kill them. Ye know that. The King and his men did. Because ye left and have now returned, the MacLeans may yet survive. Ye can bring them back here, begin anew, raise havoc with the King and show him we will not be disappeared.'

Garrick stared at him in disbelief.

'Ye will help us survive, my laird.'

'What are you talking about? We cannot claim what has been seized. I am no longer laird of anything.'

'Westmoreland has been abandoned, has it not?'

Garrick met his gaze. 'Aye. It has.'

A mustard seed of hope bloomed in his chest. Could the old man be right? Could he begin again?

Aye. He could.

Chapter Twenty-Three

'Where is he?' Brenna asked, staring out of a window buffeting the front doors of Glenhaven.

'Sister, he gave no indication of when he would return, only that he *planned* to return today. It is hardly mid-morn. Even if he left at sunrise, he would not be here by now.' Ewan shrugged into his coat and grabbed a pair of gloves.

'Where are you going?'

'To check on Montgomerie. Garrick will have my head if a piece of that stallion's mane is out of place.'

'Let me join you.' She rushed over to gather her own cloak and gloves, and they descended the castle stairs together. She slipped her arm through his and hugged him. 'I have missed you, brother.'

'Where is all of this softness and affection coming from? If I'd known all you needed was to be tossed about in a carriage and chased down to near death to make you kinder to me, I would have done it long ago.' He winked at her, and she swatted his arm.

'Hush, now. None of that is the least bit funny.'

His smile flattened. 'I know. But to make light of it makes me better able to manage it. You are my baby sister, and I adore you. The thought of losing you was unbearable. And seeing you again has brought all of us joy, especially Father. He even asked to dine with us this eve.'

'That is wonderful! You see, he will improve.'

'Bren,' Ewan started. 'He will enjoy what time he has left. I do not wish you to get your hopes up. The doctor said he is nearing the end.'

She sniffed and wiped at her eyes that were misting in the cold weather. 'Aye. I know.'

'But, for now, let us fuss over Montgomerie so the boy is in fine spirits when Garrick returns.'

'May we invite Garrick to stay? He is alone.' She began to brush Montgomerie's haunches while Ewan brought him fresh hay.

Ewan shrugged. 'Of course, but he may not wish to. I would not get your hopes up. I have never seen him in such a state, and he may feel worse after his visit to Westmoreland.'

'You are right. I just wish so many things had turned out differently between us.' She leaned into Montgomerie's side, and he nuzzled her back.

'Who says it is too late?' Ewan answered, spreading out the hay.

'He does. He cannot forgive himself for what has happened to his family.'

Ewan shook his head. 'Never stopped you before.'

She lobbed a stable cloth at him. He dodged the

towel successfully, as he always did. He threw a few rogue pieces of hay at her, and they stuck to her cloak, as they always did. She made a face at him, and he laughed.

'Up to the same old mischief, I see.'

Brenna's heart jumped at the sound of Garrick's voice behind her as he galloped up the drive.

'Glad to see you returned,' Ewan offered. 'Just taking care of your stallion, as promised.'

'Thank you.' His eyes settled on Brenna.

'I'm sure Father needs me, so…' Ewan clapped Garrick on the shoulder and disappeared, leaving Brenna standing staring up at Garrick, all words having fled her mind.

'How was your visit?' she asked, and then cringed. 'Sorry. I am certain it was horrible and yet I asked you anyway.' She plucked some of the hay from her cloak and then gave up.

'Better than I anticipated.' He dismounted and stepped closer to her. The sheer heat of him made her breath catch in her throat. The harder she tried to ignore her body's response to him, the more her body reacted.

She held her ground. 'Oh?' she asked.

'I will tell you everything,' he said, his voice dropping. 'But for now…' He took another step, and his body was a sigh away from her own. She rested her hands on his chest to steady herself. The back of his fingers slid slowly down her cheek and his eyes flared a mossy green. The man was going to kiss her. Her stomach pooled with heat in anticipation. Her palms tingled against his chest, and her heart picked up speed. What was she doing? What were they doing? This was no way to go about moving on from one another.

'Garrick, I...' She began but, before she could utter another word, he seized her lips with his own. The intensity and urgency of his kiss as his arms wound around her with purpose and ferocity nearly knocked her out of her slippers.

She sighed against his lips and kissed him back with all she had and the repressed longing and love for him poured out of her. She had missed him more than mere words. He pulled her closer, deepening his kisses, and she savoured the feel of him pressed against the length of her body. A bucket dropped behind them, and Garrick pulled away. He glanced out to the main entrance of the stable and chuckled.

'I think we may have given that poor lad more than he bargained for,' he teased.

She looked past his shoulder. The boy must have run from the place at the sight of them, as a wooden bucket sat abandoned on its side in the doorway of the barn, water still trickling onto the ground. 'Aye. Good thing he interrupted us when he did, or it might have been quite unseemly.'

Garrick smiled against her hair, and she snuggled against him. His warm, solid frame comforted her, as did the relaxed quiet between them.

'Will you stay through Hogmanay?' she asked, her words light and airy despite the uncertainty she felt about what his answer might be.

'Aye,' he answered. 'I would like that.'

She pressed a kiss to his cheek. 'Then, we shall have a wonderful time.'

His agreement was just one of the many miracles that had happened since they had returned to Glenhaven.

He pulled back and ran a hand down her hair. 'I have much to attend to this morn, and correspondence that needs to be sent out as soon as possible, but I wish to speak with you when the time is right.'

'Then, go,' she answered. 'I have some correspondence and duties of my own to complete. Father wishes to dine with us this eve. Join us if you can.'

'I wouldn't miss it.' He pressed a kiss to her cheek and jogged back to the main house, a lightness in his movements.

This was the Garrick she had known, the man she had fallen in love with. Something about his trip to Westmoreland had freed him. Just as her conversation with Father had set loose her shame and sadness. She hoped one day they would be whole enough to come back to each other again. This moment was the first step in doing that. Now she just needed to get on with the second one: working out what would make her happy so they could begin their future together as two whole people, not the fractured parts of each other they had once been.

Garrick hadn't anticipated the hum of energy he would feel in his bones after visiting Westmoreland. Seeing his mother and brother's graves and speaking with Phineas had loosened his grief. While he was a long way from having healed from their losses, the heavy ache in his chest was lighter. He still hadn't read his mother's letter, but he had the box on the chest in his guest chambers at Glenhaven. He would read it when he was ready, but he had many other tasks to tackle until then.

One of them was sending out enquiries to the nearby clans to enlist their support in rebuilding his own. Perhaps it was a risk, and not all would comply, but even if half of them supported his cause he would feel accomplished.

Phineas had agreed to continue on at Westmoreland as caretaker of the keep as well as whatever else he could manage. Garrick owed him more coin than he might ever have, but the man had agreed without hesitation. When the MacLeans were able to reclaim their home and lands, Phineas would be repaid in full, and more besides. Because of him, Garrick had hope for the future, and because of Brenna he still wanted to live it.

The hard part was beginning again. He'd never been good at dealing with failure, but he had to learn how to. He couldn't allow loss and grief to consume him as it had for so long. His family wouldn't have wanted it and nor did he. After awakening from a dormant sleep in his grief, he wished to live life with the sun on his face and with Brenna by his side.

Hours passed quickly, and before he knew it the sun began to descend in the afternoon sky. A stack of correspondence ready to be sent out by messenger teetered on the desk, and Garrick was pleased in all he'd accomplished. They would be en route to the clan lairds and elders on the morrow, and he would be ready for the next step in his plan: to learn all he could about how to reclaim his land and castle. He'd start with the books in this very library, and then with Bran himself if he was up to it. The man had a wealth of knowledge and might even know how to shorten the time it would take for Garrick to re-establish his clan.

He closed the book on the desk and ran his hand over the supple leather. If he couldn't reclaim Westmoreland and his clan, he would begin anew, perhaps even join the lost village or settle in the old MacDougall lands nestled between the Camerons and the McKennas. He would not give up on the life that had been spared in him.

Phineas had reminded him of that. So had Brenna, but he'd been too bull-headed to accept it at the time.

'This was always Moira's favourite part of the castle.' Brenna stood in the half-open doorway of the library.

He rose from his chair, stretching the ache from his back from sitting for so long. 'It is peaceful.'

'Aye.' She came into the room. 'Dinner will be within the hour. You look to have accomplished a great deal.' Her fingers skimmed over the letters and the stamped crest in the wax seals securing each of them. She smiled. 'I see you have your ring back.'

He looked down at the ring on his finger and nodded. 'When I went to Westmoreland yesterday, I saw Phineas. He gave me a box from Mother. This was within it.'

Her hand stilled and she met his gaze.

'The old groundskeeper? He is alive?'

He chuckled. 'He is. Stayed on when the duke took over, and even after when the place had been abandoned.'

She sat in the chair opposite him, her eyes wide. 'Abandoned?'

'Aye. Westmoreland sits dark and empty. He lives in the small keep and cares for the grounds as best he can. He even helped to bury the dead with your brother, father and the other soldiers they sent.' His eyes welled. 'Their kindness in giving them peace, my family peace when I could not, shall not be forgotten.'

She reached out and took his hand in her own, rubbing her thumb over his palm. 'I am so sorry. I wish I could...' She faltered 'Spare you this grief, take it from you.'

'I think I have given you enough grief from my own actions in the past, and I am grateful you still care for me at all.'

'I more than care for you, you know that.' Her eyes welled.

He squeezed her hand. 'I do. And I more than care for you, Bren. I do not wish to muck it all up as I did before. I need to find my way back to who I was before I can try to claim you as my own. I want to be the man you deserve.'

'You already are, you fool.'

He rose and pulled her to him, brushing a lock of hair from her forehead. 'I am not, but I adore you for believing so in me when I did not believe in myself.'

'I always will. I always have.'

'I did not understand it then, but I do now. I am grateful for it.'

'Are you finished with your work this eve?' she asked.

He stared at the box before him. 'There is one more thing I must do today. Will you help me with it? I am dreading it.'

Her eyes narrowed on him. 'Of course. What is it? Surely it cannot be worse than all we have been through, you and I?'

It would be for him, but perhaps if they forged it together he would survive reading the last words his mother would ever say to him.

He lifted the lid off the box and handed her the letter. When she looked at it, she frowned. 'I do not understand. It is addressed to you, not me.'

'Phineas gave it to me. It is from my mother. Her last letter. I need to read it, but I cannot bear to. Not alone.'

'Oh, Garrick.' She released a breath and ran a hand along his cheek. 'Of course I will stay with you while you read it.'

'Dare I ask you to read it to me? I do not think—' His throat tightened with emotion.

She squeezed his hand in her own and let go. 'Aye. I will read it to you.'

They settled on the settee before the fire together. She opened the letter and looked at him. 'Are you ready?' she asked, her voice far steadier and more certain than he felt.

He nodded, as he could not form any words.

She held the letter in one hand and gripped his hand fiercely in the other.

He released a breath and closed his eyes, steeling himself from the agony his mother's last words would surely bring. Silence pressed in on him and all he could hear was the mild crackling of wood in the fire and his heart thudding in his chest in anticipation.

My darling Garrick,
By now you know what has become of us and Westmoreland, and I am sorry beyond words that I could not tell you one final time how proud I am of who you are, and the glorious, steadfast man you have become. You were always the best of us, despite what you believed of yourself, and to know that you will return and breathe life back into our clan and this land once more gives me great peace.

And I know that you will see all of us in heaven, even Ayleen. I felt her pass and, whatever happened then and now, you cannot blame yourself for it. You must be the strong, good man you have always been and carry on with hope in your heart. Knowing you and raising you has been one of the most blessed gifts a mother could have ever received.
With much love,
Mother

Garrick covered his face with his hands. Heat flushed his body and emotion shook him from within.

Mother. Her last words were as eloquent and beautiful as she had always been. He sobbed into his hands. To never hear her voice again. To never see her smile again. So many moments she would miss, and so would he. All because of what—land? Money? Power?

He hated the King and all he had brought down upon his people and him. He hated himself for not having been there for his siblings and her when they'd needed him most. But, most of all, he hated how much time he had lost agonising over all of the things he could not change, and by hiding from the truth of what had.

Brenna rested her hand on his thigh and then kissed his cheek before she rose to leave.

'Thank you,' he murmured as he wiped his eyes, reaching out to touch her arm.

She paused and faced him. 'I will always be here for you,' she whispered, leaving him in the solace of his thoughts.

Chapter Twenty-Four

The days leading up to the new year passed quickly and Brenna loved the normality of it all. Father's health continued to improve despite everyone's expectations, and Glenhaven had a new whirr of life humming beneath its bones. While Moira and Rory decided not to travel to visit for Hogmanay, they promised to join them within the month to celebrate the coming year of 1744, and to bring the twins for a long overdue visit. Soon, there would be yet another McKenna to welcome to the world, and Brenna secretly hoped it would be a girl.

Garrick had made quick work of finding many of those MacLeans scattered about the Highlands and was scheming to secure a way to officially reclaim his home at Westmoreland and his lands, so his people could return and rebuild what had once been lost. Phineas had continued to care for the grounds, and Garrick had enlisted men who needed work to help set the inside of Westmoreland back to its former glory.

Rory's and Father's contacts had also hurried along

many of Garrick's requests regarding his clan's future. With the chaos of Stephen Winters' attempt to create an uprising along the Highlands still fresh in everyone's minds, the clans set aside their past differences and feuds to protect their united future. They vowed never to allow what had happened to the MacLeans and MacDougalls to happen again, no matter the cost. No other clan would perish without a fight, and thanks to Garrick the lost village would not become any larger than it already was.

Ewan had even helped Brenna in seeing to and coordinating the proper return and burial of Arthur and Roland to Oban, so their family could have the peace and finality they deserved. Her brother had even begun the tedious task of finding a wife. Although his attempts were half-hearted, he was at least trying rather than avoiding it altogether. Little by little he let the memory of his first love, Emogene, go.

The scandal with Stephen Winters had finally started to diminish as well. Moira's lengthy letters only confirmed that Brenna had made the right decision in returning to Glenhaven with Garrick weeks ago. If she'd stayed in Oban, she would have been harassed beyond reason. With every article, it seemed there were new details to be had about the complex ploy that had almost been a success in overthrowing the balance of power in the Highlands.

Once word of what had transpired with Mr Winters and the King's men—who turned out to be the mysterious M referenced in the correspondence they had discovered—had reached the streets of Oban, the story of corruption, foul play and the innocent deaths of Arthur and Roland were on the tongues of the gossips in town for weeks. More than once, McKenna and Cameron soldiers had found strangers lurking in their meadows, attempting to gain access to Blackmore to spy upon poor Moira and Rory to see how they'd fared after almost losing their sister and sister-in-law to a murderer set on creating dissent in Britain. Uncle Leo's hounds had been set upon them each time, chasing them all good naturedly from the grounds. The thought of it made Brenna laugh out loud once more.

She'd even assisted in cleaning the castle prior to the holiday and had enjoyed rustling through old closets and trunks, discovering treasures old and new. She was eager to set Glenhaven to rights, release the dirt and air out the old of the year to make room for the joy and hope of the new one to come. Moira would have balked at the sight of Brenna wearing an old gown and apron with cobwebs strewn through her hair.

Brenna smiled. She'd discovered there were many things she liked over these last few weeks, such as cleaning, that she had never tried before. She'd also realised she was good at a great deal of things as well, and one of them was throwing a blade. The man she had downed near Westmoreland had not been a fluke. She had keen aim. Slowly but surely, she would find her footing and purpose. Her worth belonged to her alone, and it seemed her father finally understood that about his daughters.

'Is this what you plan to wear to our fine dinner this

eve?' Garrick asked, pulling on one of her loose apron strings from behind. 'I do not mind it.' He winked at her.

She twirled around and playfully batted his hand away. 'Nay. I am finishing up before I get ready. I am eager to be rid of 1743 and to charge headlong into 1744, and the best way to do that is to sweep and clean out the old dirt and air before you let in the new.'

His smiled faltered. 'I am equally eager for this new year, although this year has not been all bad. I have found my way back to you.'

She slid into his arms. 'And I you.'

He peeked down the hallway and then tugged her against him, pressing an intoxicating and achingly gentle kiss to her lips.

As a maid rounded the corner, Brenna pulled away. 'Perhaps the hallway is not the best place to show me your affections.'

'When you decide where,' he whispered. 'Let me know. I'll be there.'

She laughed as he left her to continue on his way to the library, where he spent most of his days poring over books on law and property. The man she had loved had found his way back to life and to joy. His plan to re-establish the MacLeans had given him renewed purpose and hope, rather than sorrow, and she prayed that he would be rewarded for his efforts.

Garrick stood staring out at the fine spread of food, wine and family in the long banquet hall of Glenhaven. A young lass played the harp by the glowing hearth, and evergreen scented the room. All the colours of the season graced every nook of the castle, and Brenna's skill at decorating shone in all the fine details nestled in each room. Even Garrick's own chambers had been given a seasonal flare, and he could not begrudge her efforts.

He never could have imagined he would be here, dressed in his best and preparing to welcome in the new year a few months ago. Yet here he was, preparing to bring in the new year with the woman he had loved and lost and the family that had given him up for dead. While his chest ached at not being with his own family at Westmoreland, he knew how lucky he was to be here with Brenna and hers.

Phineas came over to him. 'Kind of ye to invite me, my laird.'

'You are my family. Why ever would I not? It wouldn't be the same without you here. I am glad you came.' He clapped the man on the shoulder in greeting.

Phineas dropped his voice. 'The lady was very insistent. I didn'a think to dare *not* come.'

Garrick laughed. 'You are a wise man. Miss Stewart can be quite persuasive once she sets her mind to something.'

'Aye.' The older man sipped from his tankard of ale and shifted on his feet. 'Not the same without them, sir.'

'Nay. It isn't. But there are times when I feel them with me.'

'Always.' Phineas pressed his hand to his heart.

Garrick stilled at the sheer beauty of Brenna when he spied her descending the staircase across the crowded room. Her long green gown spilled out like a liquid emerald to the floor, and her Stewart tartan was wrapped skilfully over it, accentuating every one of her curves. Her long, dark plait swung loosely down her back as she turned to chat with the other guests and her blue eyes sparkled with joy and amusement. She wove through the sea of guests, donned her cloak and headed outside.

He swore to all of the heavens that she had never been more beautiful than she was this eve. His heart thudded in his chest. It was now or never, and he wouldn't freeze this time. Not any more. He would act.

'Excuse me, Phineas,' he apologised. 'I must see to something.'

Phineas turned and chuckled as he followed Garrick's gaze to Brenna. 'Best ye do that, sir.'

Garrick cut across the room, intent on his mission.

This eve he would secure a wife.

He was the lost laird no longer, as his heart and his hope had been found.

It was almost midnight, and a new year would soon begin, yet Brenna could not shake the feeling that she'd left something from the past year undone. Perhaps it was that she should have been a wife by now. She shuddered at the thought of almost becoming Mrs Stephen Winters, and the fact that he'd almost killed her in his endeavour to upset the fragile balance in the Highlands. She started at the crunch of snow behind her and turned to find Garrick approaching, looking devastatingly handsome in his royal blue frock coat and kilt in honour of the event.

'Are you missing the days of being out in the cold huddled in a cave, Miss Stewart?'

She shook her head at him. 'Very funny.' She accepted the arm he offered. 'Care for a stroll to see the lights dancing off the meadow? You can see the villagers below heralding in the new year.' They walked along in silence and then paused, staring down at the winking lights and revelry below.

'It is beautiful, is it not?' she said.

'Aye. It is…as are you.'

She rested her head against his arm, and they watched the sights and sounds of the village below as they welcomed in 1744. The sight filled her heart with purpose and hope for the year that was to come. All because she had not given up on him, and he had not given up on her. By some miracle, they had found their way back to one another. All was right with the world and with this moment. There was nowhere else she wished to be.

'I've something for you,' he said.

Brenna faced Garrick. He held a small wooden box in his hand. Its lopsided red bow captured her attention and she smiled.

'What's this?' she asked, tilting her head to him. 'I did not bring your gift with me. It is inside.'

'It is but a small token for Hogmanay Day. I could not wait.'

'Garrick—'

'Because of you, I have hope, which I have not had in a while. I leave on the morrow to meet with Doran in the lost village to see what can be salvaged of Clan

MacLean and Westmoreland. Seems he knows a thing or two about land claim and taxes. There are also some MacLean clan members there. I hope to find a way to bring them home for good.'

Her heart skittered in her chest. 'Leaving?' She couldn't keep the sorrow from her voice. She had just got him back.

'Aye. But this time I am headed *to* a future rather than fleeing the past. You have taught me the difference.'

Why did he have to say such lovely things to her? Her limbs felt tingly and weak. He took her hands in his own and placed the box in them.

'And I hope you will come with me,' he said, his voice husky and deep. 'To begin the new year together.'

She hesitated.

'Open it.'

She untied the ribbon with shaking fingers and opened the box. Inside were two simple silver bands. A small one and a larger one.

Confused, she met his gaze.

He smiled. 'Your father has a gifted blacksmith. He was able to melt down Ayleen's cross and fashion it into two rings. While I know it is not common, I asked him to make one for you and the other for me. If you will choose me, that is.'

He knelt in the snow and took one of her hands in his own. 'I know I have made mistake after mistake and pushed you away when I should have run to you. I know I do not deserve you, but each day I will endeavour to be that man. To be the husband you deserve.'

She stared into his eyes as hot tears blurred her vision.

'Will you be my wife? Will you marry me, Brenna Stewart?'

'Aye, Garrick MacLean. I will. And I will endeavour to be the wife you deserve as well.'

He stood and recited part of her favourite Alexander Montgomerie poem, his Scottish burr rolling deep and strong:

The dew as diamonds did hing
Upon the tender twistis ying,
Our-twinkling all the trees;
And ay where flouris did flourish fair.

'Are you trying to seduce me, my laird?'

He nodded and brushed a lock of hair from her face. He leaned in close to her cheek. 'Aye. Is it working?' he asked, his breath skimming her ear and sending goose flesh along her skin.

'I'll let you know,' she murmured, meeting his lips halfway for a kiss as the snow began to fall.

* * * * *

If you enjoyed this story,
be sure to read Jeanine Englert's other great reads!

Eloping with the Laird
The Highlander's Secret Son